I don't need you....

I don't need your store. I can take care of myself, thank you very much. I don't want somebody who doesn't want me, who I can't trust. So I'll do what Aunt Clara says and make lemonade out of any sour lemon.

But thinking of Raymond Boswell as a lemon wasn't easy when she'd been so close to him putting a diamond on her ring finger. Or had that been only her fantasy?

Gloria Seely slowed her pace. It wasn't like she was going somewhere. She paused only a few steps from the mailbox at the end of the sidewalk no more than fifteen feet down from the front porch.

Maybe acceptance was in that mailbox and would put her on the interstate of life. After all, she had education, had experience. She mustn't let *them* take away her confidence.

YVONNE LEHMAN

is an award-winning, bestselling author of 50 books, including mystery, romance, young adult, women's fiction, and mainstream historical. She founded and directed the Blue Ridge Mountains Christian Writers Conference for 25 years and now directs the Blue Ridge "Autumn in the Mountains" Novel Retreat, held annually at the Ridgecrest/LifeWay Conference Center near Asheville, NC.

Books by Yvonne Lehman

HEARTSONG PRESENTS

A Knight to Remember

Yvonne Lehman

Heartsong Presents

Thanks to Cheryl Wilson, ABCCM (Asheville Buncombe County Christian Ministries) Volunteer and Special Events Director, who has worked with the homeless in the Asheville area for the past thirteen years. She met with me in a coffeehouse and graciously answered all my questions—and those I didn't know to ask—about the homeless, shelters, and volunteers.

A huge thanks to Jeff and Palette Butler, proprietors of the Veranda Café & Gifts, the best place to eat lunch in Black Mountain, North Carolina. They're located on the street that our thousands of annual tourists know about: Cherry Street. They have unselfishly let me use their recipe with the secret ingredient that fits perfectly in my story.

A note from the Author:
I love to hear from my readers! You may correspond with me by writing:

Yvonne Lehman
Author Relations
P.O. Box 9048
Buffalo, NY 14240-9048

ISBN-13: 978-0-373-48609-0

A KNIGHT TO REMEMBER

This edition issued by special arrangement with Barbour Publishing, Inc., 1810 Barbour Drive, Uhrichsville, Ohio, U.S.A.

Scripture taken from the HOLY BIBLE, NEW INTERNATIONAL VERSION®. NIV®. Copyright © 1973, 1978, 1984, 2011 by Biblica, Inc.™ Used by permission. All rights reserved worldwide.

Scripture quotations marked NLT are taken from the Holy Bible, New Living Translation, copyright © 1996, 2004. Used by permission of Tyndale House Publishers, Inc., Wheaton, Illinois 60189, U.S.A. All rights reserved.

Chapter 1

3

*H*ome.

That's where the heart is *alleged* to be.

If so, then yes, Thomas Knight had come home.

"Don't drive to the entrance," he instructed the taxi driver when they neared the hotel. "Let me out here at the sidewalk."

The driver pulled over to the curb and shut off the meter. "Enjoyed talking to you. I don't get to the suburbs often. Most of my driving is from the airport to the DC hotels and back again."

Thomas handed him his fare and tip. "Thanks. Nice ride."

"Thank you," the driver said. Ducking his head, he peered past Thomas in the passenger seat. "Nice-looking place."

Thomas nodded, got out with his backpack, and shut the door. He lifted his hand in farewell, and the driver pulled away from the curb.

Nice-looking place, yes.

Thomas stood on the sidewalk, staring at the one hundred-year-old, three-story, white Victorian structure. His gaze swept upward to the third floor that consisted of the suite with its king-sized bed, private bath, and small sitting room. A sense of longing surged through him at the windows of the room next to the suite. The hotel looked more like a welcoming bed-and-breakfast than a hotel, reminding him of the fallacy of first impressions.

Just as a book couldn't be judged by its cover, or a man by his appearance, a hotel couldn't be judged by its columns, upper balconies, immaculately groomed lawn, or budding cherry trees mingled with a background of red maples, tulip poplars, and white oaks.

A curved concrete driveway provided an entrance and an exit. He strode up the right side of the drive to the entry, bordered by a blue lavender hedge. He could almost smell the fragrance, although the blooms wouldn't appear until summer. On each side, in front of the white banisters, boxwood shrubs formed a green background for the myriad colored pansies—yellow, purple, pink, and white—growing in profusion in the flower beds.

James had been true to his word in keeping the place looking decent for the small town. The hotel had been a mecca at one time for tourists who preferred not to stay in the heart of Washington, DC, but in Silver City instead. Thomas's dad had wanted guests to feel at home, even talk to each other in the large living room, where cozy flames leapt and danced in the spacious fireplace whenever winter storms howled outside.

Stepping onto the blue-stained wooden porch, Thomas touched the knob of a royal blue rocking chair. He didn't bother looking through the glass-paneled doors but focused on the sign he'd posted there after having the utilities turned off and locks secured: CLOSED UNTIL FURTHER NOTICE.

The insides were void of human habitation. Abandoned.

Had been for over three years. The same amount of time Thomas had been…away.

No, one could not judge the insides by the outward appearance.

Mentally shaking away threatening memories of the past, Thomas turned and sat in a blue rocker. James probably stored them in the winter and brought them out in spring. Maybe passersby stopped to sit in the rockers and enjoy the scenery even though they couldn't enjoy the inside of the hotel.

Familiar cool March winds brushed his face. Fluffy white clouds skittered rapidly across the blue sky as if spring couldn't wait to make its full appearance in the nation's capital.

He felt a smile as he thought of cherry blossom time in Washington. The trees in front of him sported pink buds. With the white hotel at his back, he faced the direction of another White House. That brought thoughts of one's right to life, liberty, and the pursuit of happiness. Politicians in that capitol were supposed to ensure such rights for its citizens. Many experienced the results of such rights; but there was another side to life, others who had little opportunity to pursue much of anything.

He had pursued.

And where had it gotten him?

That remained to be seen.

He heaved a hefty sigh, pulled his cell phone from the side pocket of his backpack, and punched the first of only a few numbers in his phone.

Holding it up to his ear, he listened to the message. "You have reached the office of James B. Knight, Knight and Son, Attorneys at Law. Mr. Knight is not available at this time."

No, the elder Mr. Knight was dead.

"Please leave your name, number, and a brief message. Mr. Knight will return your call at his earliest convenience."

Thomas joked. "Not available for your own long-lost bro—"

"Thomas?"

Hearing his name spoken by James sent the adrenaline flowing faster through Thomas's veins. Whether James would feel glad or disappointed in seeing him didn't matter. They were brothers. The only remaining blood kin in the family. No, there was the extended family. James and Arlene's four-year-old, Valerie. And the baby boy Thomas had never seen.

Thomas laughed. "The one and only."

"Good to hear from you, Thomas. It's about time. What can I do for you?"

"Well, you could have a cup of coffee with me."

"Need to be a pretty darn good cup of coffee to make me chase you all over the nation. Where are you now?"

Thomas was tempted to say he was home, right there in Silver City, where his heart had always been.

"Since you're the one with transportation, what about the Silver Percolator on Main?"

"You're kidding. Right?" James's words came quickly.

Thomas scoffed. "Have I ever kidded?"

"Not in about three years or so."

They both chuckled. "Let's see," James said. "It's my break time anyway. See you there in about twenty minutes."

"Hurry up, James. I'm needing that coffee." Thomas closed the phone and heaved a deep breath. What he needed most was renewed contact with his brother. He hoped James felt the same way.

But James enjoyed the good life with a successful law firm, fine home, pretty wife, and two children. He could get along fine without his younger brother.

Chapter 2

I don't need you. I don't need your store. I can take care of myself, thank you very much. I don't want somebody who doesn't want me, who I can't trust. So I'll do what Aunt Clara says and make lemonade out of any sour lemon.

But thinking of Raymond Boswell as a lemon wasn't easy when she'd been so close to him putting a diamond on her ring finger. Or had that been only her fantasy?

Gloria Seely slowed her pace. It wasn't like she was going somewhere. She paused only a few steps from the mailbox at the end of the sidewalk no more than fifteen feet down from the front porch.

Maybe acceptance was in that mailbox and would put her on the interstate of life. After all, she had education, had experience. She mustn't let *them* take away her confidence.

Pausing at the mailbox she looked up, aware of the mid-morning chill from the wind that sent a few fast-moving clouds drifting across the blue-gray sky. *Please, God? Don't let it rain on my career parade.* That was about as close to a prayer as she got lately. A lot of prayers from Aunt Clara and Uncle Jim had gone up for her job hunt. Maybe He would answer their prayers, if not hers.

She reached the mailbox on which someone, probably Aunt Clara, had painted daisies on the side around the names Clara and Jim Dobbins. Tied to the wooden post was ivy mingled with long-stemmed coneflowers left over from last year's crop. The seeds attracted birds. They also invited butterflies and bees, which she didn't mind, although she wasn't exactly fond of spiders.

All clear. She pulled down the flap, reached inside, and slid out two bill-sized and one letter-sized white envelopes, a gardening magazine, and a supermarket advertisement with coupons and specials.

She laughed lightly. They didn't need that. Very little store-bought food here. Clara had her own little garden. Whatever grew in spring came from the community garden, organic and fresh, or was donated to the Wildwood Center. She'd been aware of the difference between eating college food or fast food and the food she ate at Clara and Jim's. And this time of year, a lot of garden-fresh food came from Clara's pantry filled with glass jars of canned goods she'd put on the shelves last harvest season.

Gloria thumbed through the mail. Yes, advertisements. Ah. The letter-sized was addressed to Miss Gloria Seely. The return address in the left-hand corner was Silver Lining Bookstore. The large bookstores in DC had told her on the spot they weren't hiring, and she wasn't about to apply at any Walkway Christian Stores. Betty Ann, the manager at Silver Lining, had said she'd send a letter to applicants. Gloria didn't think that many bookstores from this DC suburb of 30,000 or so people would have that many apply who had her education and experience, although the unemployment rate was extremely high.

Raymond, the person she didn't want to think about, had given her a glowing written recommendation. *That was the least he could do—after what he did.* She had felt a twinge of guilt when she told the manager she quit working at the store in Shenandoah Valley to come live with her aunt who broke a bone at the side of her foot. That was true, just skewed. Five weeks of unemployment passed before she told her aunt she'd quit and asked if they knew of any jobs. That's when Clara and Jim said she could stay with them while she searched for the right job. She'd stayed with them during high school and summer breaks from college until moving into an apartment with a college friend.

She stopped her finger before it could slide under the flap and make a jagged edge. She would wait and use a kitchen knife to cut a neat slit. With an ironic scoff she added to the thought—*being the competent, efficient person I am.*

Yeah, right. I quit instead of waiting to get fired, so I can't even get unemployment checks. Great move!

Feeling the cool breeze on her face and a tickle on her cheek, she lifted her hand and tucked the errant lock of hair behind her ear.

Aware of the buoyancy in her step and a rush of anxiety-ridden adrenaline, she studied the small three-bedroom house. It had a storybook look in its quaintness. Beside the entry and in front of the picture window sat a white wicker love seat with a low wicker table in front. A wicker chair filled the adjacent corner.

A riot of color blazed in the flower bed filled with paper-white narcissus, daffodils, jonquils, and buttercups. Those delicate flowers had a hearty demeanor. She walked closer and bent to smell the sweet fragrance emitted by the jonquils. Nature gave the impression winter was over and spring almost here. Maybe the winter of her life was making a change, too.

She straightened, smiling at the house, much like other homes in the neighborhood that looked cozy and welcoming. Much like her aunt and uncle who didn't mind when she slipped up and simply called them Clara and Jim, as she had done when a child mimicking her parents. They adequately replaced the grandparents she no longer had and the parents,

Ellen and Joe Seely, from whom she'd been separated much of her life.

A bond with these wonderful people had formed early. Clara said she'd felt more like a mother to Gloria's mom, Ellen, than a sister, Ellen having been an unexpected child in their mother's middle age. Now Clara and Jim pretended they needed Gloria. But she needed them more.

The screen door creaked as she opened it and walked in. The kitchen beckoned her with its aroma of peach pies baking in the oven. Aunt Clara twisted off the top of another jar of her canned peaches, ready to mix with the other ingredients for the many pies she would send to Wildwood, the local shelter, for supper.

"Advertisements," Gloria said as she laid the junk mail at the end of the countertop since Aunt Clara was elbow deep in her cooking, stirring ingredients in a huge plastic bowl. She held her envelope close to her chest. "This one's mine."

Aunt Clara stilled the spatula. "Oh honey." Her soft blue eyes in her round face, surrounded by fine white hair, held all the love in the world. "Is it from the bookstore?"

Gloria nodded. She walked over to the silverware drawer and took out a table knife, barely hearing Aunt Clara's words. "I guess that's your acceptance."

Surely it was. Hope and prayer went a long way, and Aunt Clara's prayers seemed to go right to the throne of God and get an answer.

She slit open the top and laid the knife on the table.

She pulled out the sheet of paper and unfolded it. She read aloud.

Dear Miss Seely:
Thank you for your patience in waiting for a response. We have reviewed the many applications and find you are the most qualified of all the applicants.

Gloria squealed and glanced at Aunt Clara, whose eyebrows lifted and whose eyes gleamed with expectancy. Her lips opened in a sweet smile. She nodded.

Gloria glanced at the page again.

However, we regret to inform you...

Her voice shrank as did her hopes.

...the position is no longer available. The job offer in another town for our manager's husband fell through. She will not be leaving us after all.

Gloria's voice broke on the last words. She swallowed hard and cleared her throat. "There's something handwritten here."

Sorry. You would have been perfect for this. Enjoyed talking with you.
Betty Ann

Gloria laid the letter and the envelope on top of the supermarket advertisement and dropped them into the recycle bin. Too bad there wasn't a recycle bin for a loser.

"I'm so sorry, honey. I know you need to get on with your life in your way. But you're an answer to prayer for me and Jim."

Gloria walked over to the sink and washed her hands, her back to Aunt Clara. That's what they'd said upon learning she lost her job. They invited her to stay with them since Clara slipped on some ice a few weeks ago and broke a bone on the left side of her foot. Gloria couldn't imagine that slowed her aunt down. She was a whiz even wearing that shoe boot.

But Gloria needed a place to stay until she could earn enough money to support herself. Drying her hands, she turned to Clara. "The youth planning committee meets tonight at six. Uncle Jim wants me to sit in on it." She laughed lightly. "And order the pizza, probably clean up later."

Aunt Clara nodded. "Maybe you'll be back in time for the Bible study."

Gloria shrugged. "I doubt that a youth eating-meeting will be finished in an hour."

Clara's glance held a hint of hope. "You know it's all right if you come in late."

Gloria knew that. After all, she lived here now. Jim and the youth director, Greg, worked together on youth events that involved Wildwood and the church. Since Greg couldn't be at the meeting tonight, Jim had asked her, and she knew he was only trying to make her feel needed, which she didn't.

Gloria stared down at her hands as she wiped them with a paper towel. Aunt Clara said more of her expected encouraging words. "I know Jim appreciates your help. As I do."

Gloria tossed the paper towel into the wastebasket, on top of her rejection letter. "Then I'd better get busy helping you."

They smiled at each other. Gloria turned to the table. She would help make pies and take them to the shelter. She couldn't help but wonder if a shelter for the homeless, like Wildwood, might be her home if it weren't for Aunt Clara and Uncle Jim.

She thought of her aunt saying she was an answer to prayer. Maybe she should tell Clara not to pray for her. This didn't exactly fit in with what she'd planned for her life.

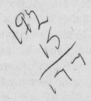

Chapter 3

Man does not live by bread alone, the Bible said.

He needs soup, too, Grandmother added.

Both quotes had appeared on the menus in the hotel dining room.

Both Dad and Grandmother had gone to their heavenly home.

Thomas walked the few blocks from the hotel to the Percolator, comparing the cool, fresh air with the memories of a putrid-smelling alley. He entered the Percolator, absorbing his surroundings, aware of what changed and what stayed the same in three years. One of the empty booths in the sandwich and coffee shop, next to the windows along one wall, beckoned him. When the waitress brought over a menu he thanked her and said he was waiting for someone.

He didn't know her. She might have been here years ago when this had been a favorite haunt, but he wouldn't have given her a second thought. Now he wondered about her life and watched for a moment to see how she handled the few customers who came in to order.

She appeared content. A man walked up to the counter and ordered a bran muffin. They exchanged light chatter, and her quick laugh sounded from behind the counter. The espresso machine churned.

Hearing a page turn, he focused on an elderly man reading a thick book, sitting in a nearby booth. Across the small room, the light click of computer keys sounded. A cell phone vibrated. He could hear breathing, perhaps his own. The sweet, pungent aroma of espresso coffee, something he used to take for granted, then had to do without, now delighted his senses.

A movement outside the window caught his eye, and he turned his head in time to watch a bullet-gray Cadillac pull into the parking lot. The car that had belonged to their dad. Thomas's heart raced as his brother climbed out and hastened around the side of the building. James stopped inside the doorway and his eyes searched.

Thomas waited for his brother's double take, then lifted his hand and scooted out of the booth. James shook his head and directed his gaze toward the ceiling for a moment. Thomas waited for whatever overture James might make. Next thing he knew he was enclosed in a bear hug, then James was arm's length away with his hands on Thomas's shoulders. "I wouldn't know you anywhere," James said.

They both laughed and sat in the booth, Thomas in his jeans and T-shirt, James in a suit and tie.

James spied the menu. "Whatcha having? Sandwich? Roll?"

At the moment Thomas just wanted to feast on the sight of his brother. James looked good. "Just coffee."

"Come on," James said. "This one's on me. After all, I haven't seen my own brother in three years."

"Same for me, James. So why not let it be my treat?" James probably thought he was completely out of money.

James lifted his hands in surrender. "Okay. We're on our own." He looked at the waitress who walked over. He nodded at Thomas.

"Regular coffee black, please."

James glanced at the sugar container. "Cream for mine, please."

"Two coffees," she said and walked away.

"You did say you were only on break, James."

James's forearms came up onto the table, and he leaned forward, his dark brown eyes boring into his brother's. "No. I said I'd come on my morning break. If you wanted me to, or needed me, I'd take the entire day off. The week."

"A month?"

James laughed. "If you needed me, yes."

Thomas nodded. He knew that was true. He watched James look out the window at the few cars in the parking lot. He was probably wondering what to say to his younger brother who had rarely listened to his advice anyway. People used to say the two of them looked alike. Not now. James had the look of a successful attorney, his dark, wavy hair conservatively cut and smoothly combed. Thomas cut his own wavy hair, strands highlighted from the sun, when he stopped to think about it or found a pair of scissors. He hadn't trimmed his beard in a while and it, too, had a few highlights.

The waitress set the cups down. Her glance quickly skimmed over Thomas then she concentrated on James and smiled. Likely, she thought James was treating a homeless man. Well, she'd be half right. He wasn't being treated, but he was homeless.

Thomas picked up his cup, savoring the scent of the aromatic black liquid. He didn't think he'd ever take anything for granted again, or at least he hoped not—not even a cup of steaming coffee. He'd learned to drink his coffee without amenities. James doctored his. He took a sip and looked over at Thomas. "You know you have a home with us."

"I know. But I'm fine."

"Fine?" James expelled a deep breath. "Thomas, I've tried not to worry if I'd ever see you again. Or get word you were found in an alley somewhere." His eyes closed for a moment. "Or if I'd never hear anything."

"Sorry," was all Thomas could say. "I didn't always have access to communication. Carrying a cell phone was asking for it to be stolen. But I called you and Frank occasionally from shelters."

Thomas watched James's gaze fall to the bruise beneath Thomas's eye that was still fresh, even deeper purple and green than it had been last night. "That's quite a colorful shiner you have there."

Thomas scoffed and shrugged a shoulder. "You think that's bad, you should see what my arms got in self-defense."

James shook his head. "So you're fighting now?"

"I said self-defense, James. I don't really fight with a man who is simply defending his home."

James's eyes questioned and his mouth opened, but no words came forth.

"His home," Thomas said, "is a particular alley and his own personal dumpster. He didn't care to share."

He laughed lightly, but James's furrowed brow indicated he didn't see the humor in it. "Thomas, where will you stay? In the hotel without electricity or water?"

"I've stayed in worse places."

James released a deep breath while reaching into his suit coat pocket. "Here are the keys to the hotel." Thomas thanked him. "At least come home and…and get cleaned up."

Thomas pinched his T-shirt and held it out. "It's amazing how clean a person can get with just a little water. My clothes aren't dirty. Just worn."

James reddened. "I didn't mean…"

"You've never had to be careful with me, James. Don't start now. We're brothers. You can insult me all you want."

That brought a familiar grin to James's face. He took a gulp of coffee and set the cup down, serious now. "I'm sorry things didn't work out the way you hoped. I thought Arlene's dad might do something for you."

Thomas didn't think this was the time to get philosophical and discuss the value of things not always working out the way you expect. He'd simply state a couple truths. "Frank said my work wasn't good enough. And the big hotels across the country weren't interested in soup. With these precarious economic times, they've cut back instead of taking on anything or anyone new."

James nodded, understanding. "This area's been hit hard." He paused a moment and looked down at his cup. He was probably thinking of their dad who had been hit hard and didn't recover.

James looked across at him then. "Several major regional companies have folded or gone to other countries. Businesses are laying off. There's a lot of out-of-work people here."

"Exactly," Thomas said. He leaned forward. "That's why I came back. I've been north, south, east, west, and to the middle states. Now it's time to check out my own backyard, so to speak. The suburbs of the nation's capital."

James looked puzzled.

Thomas felt his own sense of purpose rise. "Sometimes life surprises us, James. I've learned something valuable. Being poor means being an accident, an illness, or a paycheck away from living on the streets."

James stared for a moment as if trying to decipher that. He glanced down, picked up his cup, and brought it to his lips. He might be thinking that he hadn't gone under. He'd worked at making a living and was doing great.

Thomas picked up his own cup. No need to say what he was doing, or why. He'd done that three years ago, and it had sounded like empty words.

And to say he'd learned that failing is the most successful thing one could do at times would sound worse than empty. It would sound idiotic.

This wasn't the time to reveal that he'd planned to change the world. Instead, the world changed him. James would take that as a confession of failure. "I want to get the packages I mailed to you."

"They're in a safe place in my office. Any time you want them, just let me know and I'll get them to you." James set his cup down and looked over at Thomas with a serious expression. "Come to the house, Thomas. You know we have plenty of room. Arlene and the kids would love to see you."

"Thanks. I want to. But I have a few things to do first."

He tried to ignore the disappointment on James's face on hearing he wouldn't jump right into family life. They'd been close. They were close. But they didn't look at life the same way. "So," Thomas said, hoping to dispel the settling gloom. His gaze settled on James's wedding band. "Tell me about Arlene and the children."

James reached into his back pants pocket and brought out a wallet. He flipped to some pictures and began. Valerie, now four years old and Blake, a baby boy.

One picture was taken outside the big house in Takoma Park. A rush of joy and sorrow assaulted Thomas with a flood of memories. He'd grown up in that house and had the best life a child could want. Now it belonged to James.

Thomas grinned. James's face and manner became transformed as he showed the pictures. Yes, he was a successful, content man. Thomas was happy for him and knew that was James's characterization of the good life. But Thomas's definition of the good life was represented right there in his backpack and in the packages he'd mailed to James.

Thomas smiled at the pictures then looked across at James. "You have a good life, don't you, bro?"

James's gaze fell to his empty cup as he gave a single nod. "I'm blessed, Thomas. But I work hard, too."

"You've always been…" Thomas searched for the perfect word. It came. "Conscientious," he said.

James's shoulders rose, and Thomas knew his brother was weighing the words to discover their meaning. All it meant was fact, as far as Thomas was concerned. No condemnation. No praise.

"Well," James said suddenly, "the last I heard you were in New York."

"I gained valuable insights there," Thomas said. "There's something grand about standing and gazing up at the Statue of Liberty."

The expression in James's eyes darkened when Thomas added, "Then to look around and know that so many homeless sit huddled in the alleys." Not waiting for a response, he smiled. "And right here in DC the White House is to uphold life, liberty, and the pursuit of happiness." His voice dropped. "Yet not very far away are the slums."

Seeing the lips of his brother tighten, Thomas could almost read his mind.

James represented the city.

Thomas, the seamy side.

James took a bill from his wallet.

Thomas took a one from his pocket and placed it on top of James's five. "Can I drop you off somewhere?" James asked.

"Where I'm going is only about ten miles or so from here, so I'll walk."

"Only…ten miles?" James repeated then shook his head. "I guess that's not far when you've been walking the map of the United States for three years."

They laughed at the irony, but to Thomas it was a fact that he'd walked that much, even if it wasn't over the entire map. "I want to take a look at the Wildwood Church."

James's brow furrowed. "It's not a church anymore."

"I know."

He didn't need to say he'd occasionally had access to the news and computers. "Have you seen what they've done to it?"

James shook his head. "Our church donates; but no, I haven't had any reason to go there."

Further words seemed to be stuck in Thomas's throat about the place that to his dad had been a source of great joy and ultimate sadness. James looked as if the mention of the church was unwelcome.

But Thomas had a reason to go to the little church, now called the Wildwood Welcome Center.

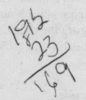

Chapter 4

"You go on home now. Before it gets dark."

Gloria heard the words, but they weren't what took precedence in her mind. Maybe it was just a shadow or a quick breeze or her imagination, but it struck concern in her heart.

She knew its source. Fresh in her mind was that a few days ago a drunken Caleb Preston was dragged from the swollen creek by Sam, his roommate. Sam said he'd talked to Caleb who sat leaned against the trunk of a big oak, hiding something at his side. His speech sounded slurred.

Later, when Caleb didn't show up for supper, Sam went looking for him and found him in the swollen creek. Somehow he'd managed to hold onto a boulder and was still breathing when Sam hauled him out of the rushing water.

Gloria didn't really know Caleb. She'd only been helping out sporadically for a little over a month, since she spent most of her time applying for work and awaiting responses. But Caleb had surprised her. Not that she expected any of the residents to break the rules and get drunk, but some of the residents had reasons to be depressed. Caleb was a young veteran. He had a wife and five-year-old son and his whole life ahead of him.

It just didn't make sense he landed in the homeless shelter to begin with.

She'd dished out food for him a few times. If she'd never seen him, she'd just think falling into the creek a horrible thing to happen. But having been so close to him, having met his wife, Heather, and son, Bobby, she felt guilt that she hadn't done something, said something.

Rumors abounded at times like that, but the worst one seemed to be that Heather was talking about leaving with Bobby and going back to her parents.

"One weak moment can wreak havoc on a person's life," Jim had said. "And sometimes a person just gives up." Compassion veiled his eyes. "Or maybe he didn't mean to fall in. His war experiences might have overwhelmed him. I can identify with that." He nodded with a sad look in his eyes. "Believe me, it's hard to forget."

Gloria knew Jim had his own war experiences but rarely talked about them. She tried to erase Caleb from her mind. But the thoughts persisted. What had he felt when he landed in the cold water? Just the thought of a spray of cool water in the shower made her shiver. She wondered if he had fallen in, or if he meant to make that plunge.

"Gloria?"

With a start, she looked over her shoulder. "Sorry. My mind was elsewhere. What did you say?"

"You need to get going before dark."

She turned and shook her head. "Uncle Jim, you know how far the house is from here?"

He stood straighter as he leaned back slightly and tried giving her a harsh look, impossible for that pleasant man. "Well, I should since I live there. Are you implying I'm old and forgetful just because I have a few gray hairs?"

She laughed. He had a few dark hairs mingled with the gray. "No. I'm saying I think I could outrun a mad dog for two blocks."

"Yes, but before you get to the blocks, there's the church parking lot that runs close to the road and that wooded area between the road and paths around the creek. You never know what wild animals might be watching and waiting."

She placed her hands on her hips. "Why don't you come with me?" She teased, using his words. "It's getting dark."

He chuckled softly. "I have a few things to do here; then I'll be in my office at the center for a little while. Anyway, I'm not worried. Not as pretty as you." His gray-blue eyes danced. "Blonds with blue eyes make a person stare, you know."

She shook her head. Her hair was a drab light brown and in her latest style, a ponytail. Her eyes looked more gray than blue to her, like his, unless they reflected something blue. That was just Uncle Jim's way. Saying complimentary things. That brought Raymond to her mind. The one person she did not want to think about.

"Anyway," he said, "I need to sweep up. How can a few kids planning their next fund-raising project manage to wreck a place so easy?"

"Just comes natural. But I have a feeling the pizza and drinks are what did it." She laughed, picked up her camera, and tucked it into her tote bag. The picture she'd taken of the youth planning team would appear in the next shelter newsletter. "See you in a little while." She left through the back and walked slowly past the Welcome Center. She didn't want to get caught up in Aunt Clara's Bible study tonight. Heather often came and brought Bobby with her. Seeing them would be even more depressing after what happened to Caleb.

Instead of turning left and walking two blocks to the house, she turned right, heading toward the trees bordering Silver Creek. Impending darkness or not, wild animals of the human kind or not, she had to know if she'd seen someone take the path near Wildwood and walk into the trees. Caleb had gone there. Another resident might get it into his mind to do the same

The sun had set. The sky was darkening. The woods shadowed the path. She walked along and her heart pounded. She hadn't been mistaken to think someone was out there.

A man stood near the oak where the whiskey bottle had been found. On the highest part of the embankment. The creek was still swollen from the spring rains. The water rushed over the boulders with a churning sound, fast-flowing toward the river.

She didn't want to frighten him, cause him to topple over into the depths where he seemed to be staring.

"Sir?" She spoke softly. He didn't move. She said it a little louder. He turned his head then and looked at her.

Shadowed, and in the dim light, he was almost a silhouette. She could make out that the tall, lean figure wore jeans and a T-shirt. He had unkempt hair and a beard. "Are you all right?"

He lifted a shoulder. "Depends on who you ask."

She didn't know if that was a joke or something serious.

She stepped closer. "I was just curious." She didn't want to say *concerned*. "There was a man who stood in that spot a few days ago."

He tucked his thumbs in his front pockets, turned his face toward her, and lifted his eyebrows. "Is that against the law?"

"Well no." Now she felt embarrassed. "He…fell in."

He took a step back and leaned against the tree. "Did he come out?"

"No. He had to be pulled out."

He looked at the water and back at her. "You think I might…fall in?"

He said that with the same tentative inflection on the *fall in* words she had used. She shrugged. "I don't know. He had come to the shelter. I thought you might have heard about him. Maybe knew him. Maybe that's why you're here."

"Would you believe I was standing here thinking about the Wildwood shelter?"

She assumed that was a rhetorical question.

"I'd like to talk with the person who manages it."

She could believe that. All bearded men weren't homeless, but she still held her stereotypical image that homeless men in alleys didn't shave. Most of the residents at the center shaved each morning. Then a strange thought occurred. A criminal returns to the scene of a crime. Maybe Caleb had been… pushed. Oh, she'd read too many of Steven James's thrillers.

She shouldn't pry too much. And once the sun sank below the horizon, darkness came quickly. "There's an attendant at the shelter. You can go in."

"Is the person who manages it there?"

"The resident assistant is a volunteer. But I can take you to the church to talk to Jim. He's director of Wildwood." Although curious about what he wanted, she didn't say she might be able to give him some information. After all, she was constantly telling herself she was a temporary fixture at a place that didn't really need her. The youth meeting proved that. Although young, they had wonderful ideas and plans.

His words interrupted her thoughts. "That sounds a lot more inviting than the cold creek water." He reached down to the base of the tree, picked up a large backpack, and shrugged into it. He adjusted the straps over his shoulders.

She didn't know the protocol in a case like this but had a strong feeling she'd made the wrong decision. Maybe she should reconsider and say he must go to the shelter and talk to the RA instead of leading him to Jim who was in the church alone. But she didn't know if this man was homeless. He wasn't exactly direct with his answers to her questions. However, she reminded herself, she'd seen Jim effectively handle a man who definitely needed help beyond that of the shelter.

She led the way out of the shadowed woods, past the Wildwood Center, and toward the large brick church where lights shone from basement windows.

Each time she glanced at him, the man looked over at the woods or switched his gaze to the center or to the church ahead of them. He was probably sizing her up, like she was doing with him.

After leaving the woods, even in the dusk she could see that his eyes were clear, despite the discoloration beneath his right eye. Otherwise his face, what little she could see of it, looked youngish; his walk was quick and agile like a person in good shape. She was told her first day at the shelter that the homeless were just people, like everybody else, and not to treat them any differently. She was trying.

But Caleb had been young and strong and seemed to be rational. He was clean-cut and intelligent. Who knew what went on beneath one's surface? And this man walking beside her, maybe he wasn't homeless but some wealthy fellow wanting to help out the center.

Sure! A guy in worn jeans and sporting a black eye.

She took a deep breath. "My name is Gloria."

He looked directly at her then, and she pushed aside the strand of hair the breeze blew from her ponytail and against her cheek. With a feeling of chagrin, she noticed his ponytail was still intact at the back of his neck. What had she come to, comparing her hair to a man's?

"Nice to meet you. I'm Thomas. Um…"

She waited, wondering what he had on his mind. When he said it, she was floored. "Are you homeless?" he said.

Her breath came out fast, almost a laugh. Normally the answer would be ready, and she'd say no, she just helped out there, and add the thought that she was a product of nepotism and charity.

For minimum wage.

Part-time.

Temporary.

But something in the way he studied her, the way he asked, made her think more deeply.

Not everyone who was homeless lived in a shelter. What,

and where, is one's home? She didn't appreciate his reminding her that she would have to answer that question at some point.

But she shouldn't be discussing her personal life with… with a pony-tailed male stranger.

Tilting her chin upward, she looked into his dark, probing eyes. She tried to make her words sound flippant, as he had earlier. "Depends on who you ask."

"Mmmm." A smile moved his beard.

The sound he made, and the single nod of his head, gave her the impression he had read her mind.

Chapter 5 3

Thomas put his hand on the doorknob but didn't turn it. He glanced back and watched Gloria walk away.

Judging by the jeans and shirt she wore, along with the sneakers, perhaps she lived nearby and had simply taken a walk along the creek. But she'd seemed deliberate about being there, talking to him, and leading him back toward the church.

The homeless had many kinds of eyes—helpless, hopeless, vacant, frightened, downcast, hopeful, thankful. Hers seemed concerned. Perhaps she was close to the man who fell into the creek. Although she said someone pulled him out, that didn't mean he was alive. Thomas felt he should have been more sensitive to her.

But his mind had still been as full of memories as the pad he'd sketched in all afternoon. He'd sat on the other side of the creek until shadows began to creep over his pad and the path.

Now he watched her walk off in the direction opposite the center, across the church parking lot and toward the residential area. Although he'd detected a sadness about her, she'd been cordial.

Until he asked if she were homeless.

Interesting.

She apparently knew there was more th...
homelessness. He'd known a few people who o...
houses, but their lifestyles indicated those were not ho...

Turning toward the door, he opened it, and his gaze fell
upon a scoreboard on the wall opposite him. Prominent on
each side were basketball goals on a board attached to the
ceiling. A man's voice said, "Welcome, friend."

Thomas stepped inside, closed the door behind him, and
observed an older but spry-looking man walking toward him.
"Name's Jim," the man said, shifting the broom into his left
hand and extending his right one. Thomas gripped it and exchanged a firm handshake.

"I'm Thomas. A young woman said you direct the Wildwood Welcome Center."

"Well, at least I oversee that it's directed, which means I'm
able to delegate authority and see that others do their jobs. It's
too much for one person." He tapped the broom handle. "As
you can tell, I'm sort of a Jack-of-all-trades."

Thomas had a feeling he was probably master of many,
contrary to the negative connotation of the adage.

"Come on in. Have a seat." Jim reached over where folding
chairs were stacked against the wall and brought one forward.

Thomas quickly reached for another chair and unfolded it.
They sat on the only furniture set out in the room marked off
with lines for a basketball court, obviously a multipurpose
room. Jim propped the broom handle against his leg.

Most of the room looked cleanly swept, although a few
streaks of dirt lingered near where they sat. Paper plates and
foam cups were visible in an open plastic bag against the wall.
Returning his gaze to Jim, he had the feeling that man likely
could see beneath one's facade.

"How can I help you?" Jim asked.

"Well…" Thomas thought a moment. How much should
he say? "That's what I was about to ask you."

The man's gaze remained steady as he simply waited for

...xt. He might well be thinking that
...mental problem they didn't handle

...ward slightly. "The way you can help
...be a self-imposed homeless volunteer."
...omeless volunteer," Jim mused, studying
him ... y eyes that seemed to turn bluer as a grin
touched ... "What do you mean by self-imposed?"

Thomas didn't think it wise to mention the hotel where he
could find plenty of blankets that would keep him warmer
than he'd been during the nights he'd spent in alleys. But he
could mention the better option. "I have family in the area.
A brother with a wife and two children, but I'd rather not im-
pose on them."

Jim nodded, as if understanding, but a question remained
in his eyes. "The men help out where and when they can but
none have ever asked in quite that way. We usually tell the residents what we expect." He paused a moment. "Just what are
you wanting? What does 'homeless volunteer' mean to you?"

"It means I'd like to be one of the homeless for a while,
but I want to be free to come and go when I'm not needed."

Jim's eyes held doubt. "Without any questions?"

"No, I wouldn't say it that way. If you need to know, I'll tell
you. But I don't want anyone at the center to know about my
personal life. It's nothing…" He began to say more and caught
himself for a moment and grinned. "Nothing I'm ashamed of.
I'm not in trouble. Not addicted to anything."

Strange, how his mind worked. No, if his obsession was
harmful to anyone, it would be only to himself. Might cause
James a little distress, but he'd get over it.

Jim seemed to study him the way Thomas studied people's
faces, the ones that ended up in his sketch pad. "All I have
right now is something temporary. At least I hope our resident will be able to return."

Thomas wondered if that resident was the man who *fell* into the creek.

"Temporary is all I need." *Famous last words* came immediately to mind. If he'd learned anything, it was that anyone, perhaps everyone, could be one step away from hard times.

Just as Jim opened his mouth as if to ask another question, a cell phone rang. Jim slid it from his shirt pocket. "Excuse me," he said, with a worried look on his face. "It's my niece."

Chapter 6 7

Gloria had to call. She couldn't bear it if she caused any trouble. "Uncle Jim?"

"What's wrong?" he said quickly.

"Nothing, I hope." Gloria sighed. "I sent a man to see you, but maybe I should have sent him to the shelter. Is—is everything going all right?"

He laughed lightly. "You did the right thing. Everything's fine. Are you home yet?"

Now it was her time to emit a small laugh. "The house is in sight."

"Good. Tell Clara I'll be there shortly."

Gloria returned the phone to her tote. Cars were parked in the driveway and two at the curb. She reached the house and walked up onto the porch. Light shone from the living room window, and she could see Clara with a Bible on her knees and several women sitting on the couch and in chairs. Bobby lay a few feet away, near the corner, stretched out on his stomach, coloring a picture with much more force than necessary. Keep that up and he'd wear holes in the paper, maybe the carpet.

His head raised and impatient eyes looked toward his mother. Gloria stepped back quickly lest he see her. Going around to the back would be like sneaking in, and they'd probably hear her anyway. Rather than sit in the light shining onto the wicker settee, she turned and sat on the shadowed step.

She'd hoped the meeting would be over by now. That was one reason she told the young people to go on home and let her take care of the cleanup, what little of that there had been. Toss a few pizza boxes, wash off a knife, and clean any crumbs. They'd deposited their own plates and cups into the trash bag, and two of the boys folded the bendable legs and propped the table against the wall.

As substitute event planner of the evening, taking Greg's place, any anxiety about her role proved unfounded. The young people obviously cared about the residents, and some of them volunteered an hour or so during the week. Before they left, they'd thanked her, as if she'd done more than listen and approve their plans.

She really didn't do enough to get paid and often felt guilty because of the volunteers who were so caring. She could enjoy it more if her small savings had not been depleted and she had not needed to use the small salary for personal items like gas for the car and—

A bevy of voices interrupted her thoughts. She stood when the porch light snapped on and the front door opened. Singles, ranging from early twenties to one woman in her seventies, began to pour out onto the porch.

She was greeted warmly, and the older woman said she missed her but Clara had said she was at an event-planning meeting. "You're such a great help to Clara and Jim," Marge said with warmth in her face and voice. "And the shelter."

Marge patted Gloria's arm and carefully walked down the steps, holding onto the railing.

Gloria heard Bobby's whine before she opened the screen door and walked inside. "I don't wanna go home. I want my daddy."

Heather looked helpless as she spoke to Gloria. "I hoped I could talk to you for a minute, but I'd better get him home."

By this time the boy's lower lip was out and his eyes blazed defiantly.

"Please, honey," Heather said. "Be sweet, now. It's your bedtime."

Staring at her, he wadded up the paper he'd been coloring.

"If you two want to talk…" Clara said, her eyes questioning, and Heather nodded. "I have another idea." She didn't look at Bobby. "I've been wanting to watch my new VeggieTales video, but I don't suppose anybody else wants to."

"I do. I do," Bobby said. "Don't wanna go home and go to bed."

Clara was nodding, so Heather released a sigh of relief. "Well, I suppose I could let you stay up a little later."

The defiance left him. "Oh boy!"

"But first, pick up your crayons and coloring book." He did and Heather looked greatly relieved.

"I'll just grab a sweater," Gloria said when Heather picked hers up and slipped her arms into it.

"Popcorn?" Clara was asking as Gloria and Heather walked out the door, and Bobby's "Oh boy!" rang out again.

"I think I'm too easy on him," Heather said when they reached the yard. "But everything's turned upside down since Caleb came home and left again." She looked around. "Shall we walk down to the playground?"

Gloria nodded. The street was well lit with sidewalks on both sides. She and Heather spoke to a couple sitting in a swing on their porch. The evening had only a slight chill in the air. The moon was visible, but no stars shone yet in the light gray sky.

Both were quiet. Gloria felt the two of them were as different as the sound of their shoes. What could Heather want to talk to her about? They walked two blocks and reached the playground at the back of the elementary school. That, too, was well lit and considered quite safe. She'd rather wander along the path by the creek, but much of it was secluded and not recommended for a single female's stroll at night. Jim said it used to be a favorite walking place until the church was turned into a shelter. Some people feared the homeless.

It disheartened Gloria to hear Clara talk of how different times were now than when she was growing up and the world seemed a safer place. "But," she said reluctantly, "you do have cell phones now if something goes wrong. That helps."

Gloria thought of her silent cell phone now. Yes, she could call out, but she rarely received a call anymore. Raymond used to call... .

"How's this?" Heather pointed to the swings.

Gloria nodded, and they sat in swings next to each other, holding onto the chains. If Heather wanted to thank her for going with Clara and Jim to see Caleb when he was at the hospital, she could have done that back at the house. She looked over at the dark-haired woman whose eyes took on a helpless look, like when Bobby hadn't wanted to leave Clara's.

"I wanted to ask how in the world you do it," Heather said.

That was puzzling. "Do? What?"

"Handle your life so well. I know you lost your job, but you seem so content to live with your aunt and uncle."

Content? Where did Heather get that? But she could be honest about one thing. "It's not hard living with Clara and Jim. Nobody could be more loving than they. Actually, I feel more comfortable with them than my parents. Their home is like my home. When my parents go on furlough, they stay with Clara and Jim or a church mission house."

Heather nodded. "That's what I wanted to know. You see, my parents want me and Bobby to come live with them. Since Caleb isn't with us, and I don't know if he will ever be, I know it would be good for Bobby. But they already belittle Caleb. I don't think we'd ever get back together if I go live with them. You see, Mom had an alcoholic dad, and the thought of drinking sets her off. But I'm hoping Caleb will change. I mean, not just change but get help. He needs help. He watched his best buddy get blown apart by a land mine. He drinks because of his war experiences, not just for the alcohol." She shook her head. "That doesn't make sense, does it?"

Gloria wasn't sure what to say. "I think it might. I guess it's like Bobby wadding up the picture he colored. It's not about the picture and it's not about you. He wants his daddy." She paused. "And you want him, too."

Heather nodded the whole time Gloria made that speech. She did pray on the way to the playground that God would give her the attitude and words she might need, or just a listening ear. But she had a feeling her understanding how Heather felt had something to do with Gloria having gone, seemingly overnight, from feeling as though she had answers to just the opposite.

And, too, Gloria lived with some very wise people. Besides that, she empathized with Bobby, who longed for his dad. She knew what it was like to want your parents, but they were off in a foreign country helping other people's children. At that thought guilt, as usual, twisted her insides. She immediately apologized to God. That was no way to honor your parents who were just doing God's will.

At least they knew God's will for their lives.

She didn't, for her own.

But the more Heather talked, the worse Gloria felt. Particularly when she said, "So would you advise me to go live with my parents or ask friends to take care of Bobby and try to find a job? Or go to a homeless shelter for a while until I know how Caleb is going to come out of this? You see"—her voice softened and she batted at the moisture forming in her eyes—"I know Caleb isn't bad. He's just had a bad time."

The first thing that popped into Gloria's mind was the shelter's grace and mercy plan. If a resident broke the rules he had to leave. He would be directed to whatever place he needed to go for help and could return to the center after thirty days. His room or bed would be waiting. If the situation warranted it, his indiscretion was forgiven, and he could again call the shelter his home.

"The church has offered to help me stay in the apartment until we see how things go with Caleb. But…" Heather hesitated. "That's charity."

Gloria didn't know how she could say things to others that she didn't apply to her own life. But she knew the right words. "That's faith, hope, and charity, Heather. Charity is love." She felt very much like a hypocrite.

Gloria didn't know enough about Caleb or the situation. Even if she did, only Heather should make such life-changing decisions. Gloria's own decisions obviously hadn't been too sound at times. Fortunately, she had the presence of mind to say, "Let me get back to you. I will pray and think about it."

"Thanks." Heather breathed a sigh of relief and some of the distress left her face. "I admire the way you just pitch in and help at the shelter. Caleb thought the world of you. And you have a lot of faith."

Gloria tried not to act surprised. Heather was seeking her advice. She didn't want to mess this up, too. "Well, sometimes it's the grain-of-mustard-seed kind."

Heather nodded as if she understood that perfectly. "Well, you know a lot about the Bible." She looked down at her hands on her lap. "I wasn't raised in the church."

"You're doing the right things in attending Bible studies and coming to the single's class. By the way," she said as a thought flew into her mind, "why do you come to the single's class?"

Heather returned her hands to the chain holding the swing and used her feet to sway gently back and forth. "When Caleb was away, I didn't feel comfortable in the couples' class. I'd see the husbands and wives together, and I'd start missing Caleb instead of keeping my mind on the lesson. My thoughts were negative, and I'd get scared, too, wondering if he'd make it back to us." She sighed and stopped her movement. "A couple of the women and I exchanged babysitting, but their reason was usually so the couples could go out together. I couldn't tag along with a couple to go see a movie, but had to find a single girl."

A sound, as if she were embarrassed, slipped from her throat as she rubbed her hands together. "I've even gone to a movie with—with Marge."

Gloria couldn't help but emit a small laugh. "Now that sounds like a great idea. If anyone is young inside, it's Marge."

Heather laughed. "You're right. Hey, maybe the three of us could go to a movie together."

"Sure, why not?" Gloria pasted on a smile. What was she getting herself into? She needed to find a job. Then she had another idea. "Aunt Clara has been wanting another volunteer to help in Vacation Bible School, teaching the ten- to twelve-year-olds. Now that's where you can learn a lot about the Bible. I learned more from the lessons planned for that age than any other time. Help me teach."

"I always wanted to teach." She sighed into the night that had grown darker. Shadows crept across the playground. A dog barked. One car drove into the neighborhood beyond them. There was the sound of distant traffic, but for the most part it was a quiet, peaceful evening. "But I left college after two years to get married before Caleb went off to boot camp. Later on, I was pregnant. Even later, he was sent to the Middle East… ." She lifted her hands as if that were an end to everything.

"There's still time. You're younger than I am."

She shrugged. "Not by much. And like you indicated, Marge might be younger than either of us."

Gloria agreed, and a gust of wind sent a shiver through her body.

Heather stood. "We'd better get back. That video has probably been played several times by now." She looked down at Gloria. "Thank you for taking time to talk to me. That helps so much. And I think you gave me the answer."

"I did?" Gloria stood and flexed her fingers, which she'd wrapped too tightly around the chain. "What was it?"

Heather laughed lightly. "Well, if you're serious about me helping in Bible school, I can't very well go to my parents. They live in another state."

"Oh well. I meant if you stay here."

Heather nodded. "I know. And I know you're right in saying you need to pray and think. I guess I do, too. Your listening to me means so much. There aren't many people I can open up to."

Later that night, Gloria lay in bed thinking about Heather's words. How could she have given the impression she knew anything when her own life was such a mess? She would pray, for all of them. But her prayers seemed to have become more a pleading, or a hope instead of anticipation of a good response.

One of the options Heather spoke about was taking Bobby and living in a homeless shelter. Gloria could identify with Heather's situation. Of course Gloria could be glad she didn't have a child to take care of. But she knew the embarrassment of being a grown woman yet having to depend on someone else for your basic needs. Heather must feel abandoned, after having waited all those months for her husband to return.

Gloria had felt homeless many times through the years when separated from her parents. No matter how much you loved them or how grateful you were to be living with your relatives, it didn't mean you weren't…homeless.

She wished that mystery man she'd found down by the creek, whoever he was, hadn't asked if she were homeless.

Chapter 7 4

"Could you give me a little information about the center?" Thomas asked.

Jim obliged. "It's for men only, and they live here until they find a job or leave by their own volition, or need a different kind of facility. This is a permanent home for a few of them. It's sponsored mainly by this church. But other churches, individuals, and businesses donate."

"If you allow me to use that empty bed, I'll be glad to work for it."

Jim's smile dented his cheeks with character lines. "You don't have to work to stay in the shelter. It's free. But we expect a man who is able to go out and try to find work. Or to take classes that give them a skill." He paused, and his intense eyes studied Thomas for a long moment. "First the interrogation."

Thomas tried to control the grin that threatened to come onto his face. This would be Jim's way of discovering by a man's reaction if he'd recently walked out of jail or prison. The center was a home as well as a shelter, not just a place where one came for a meal or one night's lodging.

Thomas nodded, as if to say go ahead.

After Jim's intense look, he smiled. "Normally, there's a questionnaire to fill out at the center. Nothing too personal. We don't ask a lot of questions here, but I do ask if you want to tell me anything about your situation, other than just facts. We know the basic physical needs."

"I understand. I've stayed in shelters before. I've been away for three years. But I grew up around here. And I've come back. I hope to stay."

"So you need a place to stay while you're looking for a job," Jim said instead of asking.

Thomas thought he could tell this man more than he could tell James, but was there really a reason? Maybe later on. But he didn't want to lie. And he didn't really *need* anything this man had to offer. He just wanted it.

"Like I said, I've returned after being away for a while. I'm strong, healthy, and willing to do any job that needs doing for a bed in the shelter."

"You're a handyman?"

Thomas grimaced. Might as well be honest right up front about something that could easily turn obvious. "Probably not as handy as most of the residents. But I know how to ask others to give me a hand when something is broken or stops up or drips. In college I was good with computers, but I'm sure technology has changed a lot in three years. I can't do intricate things. Never put a roof on but could if someone showed me how. I've taken a few culinary courses, got lessons from the best cook anywhere. Have a degree in business ed but haven't used it." He didn't think it would mean anything to say he'd minored in art and spent a summer in Paris. "I can sing a little."

Jim laughed. "Now the singing we could use. Most of the time, the men have to put up with mine."

That intrigued Thomas. He nodded. "You sound like you'd be a baritone."

Jim shrugged. "Whatever the note requires and a few not required. Maybe some that should be banned."

Thomas liked the way the man's eyes danced. Since he admitted to music he'd probably be receptive to other arts. He could share a little with this man. "I'm basically a painter—"

He stopped when Jim started laughing. Jim apologized. "Sorry."

Thomas felt heat in his face. "That's okay. I know I sound boastful or delusional."

"To say the least."

Thomas grinned. "I could take that broom and sweep out the rest of this room."

"Just this section here, near the kitchen." Jim kept his hand on the broom handle as he glanced around the walls. "The church is sponsoring a job fair later this summer. This room we call a fellowship hall and basketball court could use a touch-up in spots. Spruce it up a little. Our kitchen at the shelter could use a fresh coat of paint, too. You did say you paint?"

Thomas opened his mouth to say that's not the kind of painting he meant. But he slowly closed it. Surely he could paint walls a solid color, although he'd probably do a better job painting a mural.

Thomas listened to Jim telling him the rules. Be in by 6:00 p.m. unless there's a good reason documented or permission given. In rooms by ten o'clock and doors locked. "We provide three meals a day for our residents and sometimes other homeless or needy come in for a meal."

There were different kinds of shelters and homes with different rules. One thing remained the same. The people in charge and volunteers cared deeply about their brothers in need.

All the while, Thomas made mental sketches. Mainly his mind took in this man, sitting in a church basement after dark in a folding chair with a broom against his leg, talking to another man about helping him out. This elderly man with thick, peppered-white hair, a large nose, rugged skin like he spent a lot of time in the sun, bushy eyebrows, a furrowed brow, creases at the corners and beneath his eyes. Kind, cool gray-blue eyes. Inquisitive eyes. Intelligent eyes. Eyelids slightly droopy with the sagging skin of old age or the fatigue of helping others all day. He knew this kind of man. He respected this kind of person.

Thomas mentally photographed the man's face. A face, not so much of age but of character. Some men grew old. Some revealed character. That face would end up in his sketch pad, along with a written description, before the night ended if Thomas got the chance.

He realized Jim stopped talking and still seemed to be sizing him up. Perhaps Jim's wisdom revealed a spiritual discernment or came from years of observing the needy. And he'd have to be alert for the mentally ill, too. If Jim knew what he was really doing, he would probably be like James and think he didn't have all his mental marbles in place.

Jim leaned toward him. "You mentioned culinary courses." His eyes brightened. "We could use a cook. My niece helps since my wife broke a bone in her foot, but to tell the truth she can't cook worth a doodle. 'Course, anybody can open up a store-bought can, and the hungry appreciate it. But my wife and me, the church members, and the community like to think a homeless down-on-his-luck kind of person deserves as good a meal as a wealthy person."

"My sentiments exactly," Thomas said.

Jim held out the broom. "Okay. You can start sweeping, then we'll go find that bed."

While Thomas swept the floor, his mind focused mainly on the cooking. He'd love to get back into the kitchen. But Jim mentioned his niece. That could present a problem. A man might be king of his castle, but he had learned from his grandmother that a woman was queen of her kitchen.

Even if it was in a homeless shelter, Jim's niece was likely a middle-aged woman who might not take kindly to a man telling her how to run her kitchen.

$$192$$
$$47$$
$$\overline{145}$$

Chapter 8

Although Gloria and Jim were running later than usual, Clara insisted they eat because she wanted their opinion on her Southern cream biscuits.

"Sounds yummy," Jim said. "Like everything you make."

Jim looked at Clara with love in his eyes that made Gloria wonder if Raymond had ever looked at her that way. No, she didn't think so. But maybe that's because, contrary to her expectations, she and Raymond hadn't had a lifetime together. Anyway, she was glad Clara liked the little countertop recipe book Gloria had gotten from the bookstore where she'd worked and brought with her when she moved in. That was the least she could do, knowing Clara loved cooking.

After the yummy breakfast, she and Jim walked the few blocks from the house, past the church parking lot, and toward the center. She wondered at his sudden faraway expression and looked ahead, following his gaze. The big cherry tree at the right side of the church had more pink blossoms than yesterday. She could readily see why anyone would be enthralled by the tree's perfect silhouette against the clear blue sky.

"I need a picture of that." She took the camera from her

tote, used the zoom control, and snapped several pictures, then showed them to Jim.

"You're amazing."

"The camera does it."

"Not without your hands and eyes, it doesn't."

Ever since Jim had seen her take pictures with her phone and asked about it, she admitted photography was a hobby. He said she might take pictures of those who applied at the shelter and at some of the special events. He said his hand shook a little and sometimes he left off the tops of heads and you wouldn't know if the person was bald or had a full head of hair.

She returned the camera to her tote. "You might not remember this, Uncle Jim, but you and Aunt Clara gave me a camera for Christmas when I was ten." She saw a spark light up his eyes. "It's been a hobby ever since."

"I do remember seeing you with a camera through the years. But frankly"—he ducked his head and looked sheepish—"I don't remember it being a present. Clara did most of the buying for you and Jenny."

"Don't feel bad," she said, "that was the year the presents were mailed because you had the flu. I was so scared and prayed for you all the time and thought if I took pictures that would make God see I meant every prayer."

He nodded. "So that's what made me better. And that's why you're here now taking pictures of people at the shelter."

Gloria laughed. "You have a way of putting things, Uncle Jim."

He nodded again. "I'm joking in a way. But in another way, I believe when we love the Lord and try to do His work, everything in our life happens for a reason. There are no coincidences."

She knew her glance at him was as skeptical as her thoughts. "So the reason Aunt Clara picked out that camera fifteen years ago is so I could take head shots of homeless people in a shelter."

She said it as if it were true instead of a question. She shook her head but smiled at him, not wanting him to think she was criticizing him. In the back of her mind, she doubted coincidence put her here. Losing her job and boyfriend is what did it. She'd already heard about some of the *coincidences* that brought men to Wildwood.

Jim's thumb and forefinger played with his chin in that familiar way of his, as if anticipating what went on in her mind. "People end up at shelters for many reasons, and all that can be debated and discussed," he said. "But the important thing is whether a person lets it defeat them or looks for the blessings."

Blessings?

She didn't see how her situation could be a blessing. Oh, being with Clara and Jim was wonderful. But she was in her midtwenties, single, and unemployed. She hadn't deliberately made a bad choice, except…throwing a fit and quitting her job on the spot. That wasn't a decision, however, just an emotional reaction.

She needed to get her focus off herself and focus on that perfect picture of an ideal little church, now a shelter, ahead of her. When she'd come here last month, snow covered the ground. Now bushes burst with new growth and flower beds shouted spring with early blooms. Grass gave the yard a green blanket. The steeple still dominated the ridge of the roof, pointing to the heavens.

Jim stood aside while she snapped pictures. He used to preach to congregations about how to live for the Lord. Now he showed others every day how to be a servant for the Lord.

Seeing he had gone over to the wooden glider beneath a shade tree, she followed and sat beside him, making sure the tote holding her camera lay secure beside her.

He pushed with his feet. The glider swung gently in tune with the music of the morning, his gaze taking in the beauty of the setting bathed in early morning sunshine. After a moment, he mused, "The perfect place for one to find shelter."

She could agree with that. "How do they know to come here?"

When he didn't answer immediately, she thought he was more in tune with the setting than her words. After a moment he began to sing, "Go tell it on the mountain."

Okaaaaay. She knew part of the answer. Some were church members who had fallen on hard times. A car wreck had left one man unable to think clearly enough to work, but he was slowly improving. Caleb had difficulty adjusting to life after war and turned to alcohol, which his wife refused to deal with. At first she'd thought all the residents were church members or local people. She later discovered they were not. Some came from DC, and some wandered there from other places.

After a moment, Jim quit singing. "Hon," he said, "your question gave me the theme for my next Bible class. Not just for the men here, but for the church." He nodded. "Go tell it on the mountain."

Gloria spread her hands, indicating the setting. "Are you trying to say I should return to the Shenandoah Mountains and tell how pretty it is here?"

He chuckled. "The key words are *go tell it*."

She shrugged slightly, and he grinned. "Word gets around," Jim said. "One homeless person tells another about places where they might go. They share the information."

Gloria got the message and sat quietly, listening to him mentally and verbally preparing his Bible study. "That's what we as Christians are to do. Freely, openly share that Jesus is the answer to our sinful state and our spiritual need."

He glanced at her. She smiled. "Go on."

"Thanks," he said. "I'm on a roll." He looked up at the morning sky then ahead as he continued. "As you know, some of our residents are long-term, and a couple are lifetime. But even with those living on the street who only go to shelters during freezing nights—don't say they're too timid to tell others about a shelter. Don't say they're not eloquent. No. They tell other homeless where to go for their physical needs." He gave a hefty sigh. "Ah, that we should be so bold to tell others about one's eternal needs."

"Good sermon."

He nodded. "Now, if we will just do it."

She stood. "What I'd better do right now is get to work."

"Don't worry about that. I happen to know the director and just might put in a good word for you."

She hugged his arm, and they headed for their duties of the day. She knew he was using the royal we, including all believers, when he said we should tell others. But it made her feel inadequate.

Who was she to tell anybody how to live or what to do with their spiritual life?

She wasn't exactly a great example of success.

Chapter 9

Thomas hadn't felt so euphoric in…well, over three years. Even longer really, since there'd been sickness and death in his family even before he began his journey of self-discovery and God-discovery. Oh, he had known God already to some extent, but not as the master of his life.

But when he walked into the little church last night, his heart lurched. So much the same, and yet so different, as when he'd come here with his family. He'd been a boy when they came at homecoming time and listened to a sermon that was followed by everyone gathering around doors set across sawhorses and laden with food. They called it picnic-on-the-grounds, but it had been a feast.

Chicken legs and chocolate cake had been his favorites, cooked by his grandmother, the best cook in the world. She started him cooking by letting him mix dough while he was still in a high chair. Before dismissing for the picnic, the congregation sang about the little *white* church in the dale.

This morning, Thomas had awakened to someone singing that song, although that person's little church was brown. Thomas and his dad had sung that song when he was a boy. That was when he'd learned to bellow out a song. He sat up in Caleb's bed and looked across at Sam, who was making sounds like a combination of a moan and a yawn. Must be his wake-up ritual.

"Who's singing?" Thomas asked.

Sam blinked and reached for his glasses. "That's the RA." He laughed. "We've got a few singers around here."

Thomas recalled Jim mentioned his singing last night.

Sam rose and swung his legs off the side of the bed. He chuckled. "Just be thankful this isn't wintertime and still dark. He'd be singing 'This Little Light of Mine' and shining a big ol' flashlight in your eyes if you overslept. Getting up time is six."

Thomas thought that a fine way to wake up. Not with a flashlight in the eyes, but with singing. He felt like doing it himself.

He slipped into his jeans and shirt, then his shoes, again grateful they hadn't been stolen. Of course he hadn't expected that, but the thought had been present during the past years—from experience.

"Sleep well?" Sam asked.

Thomas laughed. "Better than in a box."

"That's for sure. We have it good here."

Homeless people didn't generally talk personally or ask many questions. But this was different from an alley. This was home to most of these men. What he and Sam talked about last night was the young man who fell into the creek. Thomas could tell Sam had taken a real liking to Caleb.

Thomas went on down while Sam was still getting into his clothes. As soon as he reached the bottom of the stairs, he hurried through the hallway and to the former sanctuary. A sign about classes and their times hung on the door. Stepping inside, Thomas smiled. The big, rustic wooden cross still hung there on the back wall. The pews were padded now. He walked on in, sat for a moment, and offered a silent prayer of thanks. Thanks that this felt like coming home although it had never been his home church. Just the place where he'd visited with his dad and had sometimes attended services with his grandmother when he was a young boy.

The stage and podium were there, a desk on one side, a table behind it, and a bookcase on the wall opposite the desk. Looked like a church classroom.

His grandmother would like this. He'd listened to her story of being baptized in that creek on a cold November day and how her heart had been warm ever since. She'd raised his dad in this church.

She'd complained about church buildings sitting empty most of the time. Maybe that's what had spurred his dad to action.

Hearing voices, he left the sanctuary and walked down the hall and into a dining room separated from the kitchen by a long countertop. He stood aside and observed volunteers chattering away and busying themselves with taking food from the refrigerator and the pantry, getting dishes out of a cabinet, and rattling silverware while taking it from a drawer.

Residents sauntered into the dining area and milled around near the countertop, all seeming comfortable with each other. A hefty woman yelled out in a hefty voice, "Sausage and eggs and pancakes this morning." She held a big spatula. "Better come on up and say if you want scrambled, fried, syrupy, or what."

He'd been in shelters where a person could pick and choose the prepared food, but not one where you gave your order and it was cooked on the two stoves. But this was more a residence. He liked that.

Several hurried over, as if they'd go hungry otherwise. The woman must be the niece Jim had mentioned. The men were saying, "Morning, Lois." "How are you this morning, Lois?" "Thanks, Lois." So he figured her name must be Lois.

A clean-cut guy, maybe in his early twenties, wearing a short-sleeved white shirt and slacks, leaned against the far end of the countertop. He wasn't helping in the kitchen nor joining in with the residents.

Their gazes met and the young man walked up to Thomas.

"Morning." He extended his hand. "Greg here." Thomas shook his hand and told him his name. "You new here?"

"Came in last night."

"I'm the church's youth minister."

Thomas nodded. He didn't think he needed to say he wasn't exactly a youth, being twenty-eight. "Glad to meet you."

Thomas usually detected that moment when a person feels unsure what to say to a homeless person. But Greg seemed to have a confident, friendly manner about him and plunged right in. "The church youth plan a few events for the center, so you'll probably be seeing some of them and me around here at times."

"Sounds good," Thomas said. "Thank you."

Sensing Greg had finished, Thomas looked over where the workers and volunteers were busy with breakfast. "Lois!" he called as he rushed around the countertop while everyone stopped what they were doing and became like wide-eyed snowmen, frozen in their spots. "That man said pancakes. Let me show you what he means," he said with an authoritative voice.

Thinking she was about to hit him or somebody would put him in a headlock, he grinned. "You're too pretty to be slaving over that hot stove anyway." She did look prettier when her skeptical eyes lit up a little like she'd give him the benefit of the doubt.

He took the spatula in his hand, wondering if he was taking his life in his hands. "Let's get rid of this little rubber saucer." He scooped up her pancake and put it on a nearby plate. "Now," he called, glancing around. He spied the cereal and fruit display. "Banana pancakes coming up. Put your order in now."

Several did, wondering when the hands-on-hips-Lois might

throw something at him and sit on him. He reached for the bowl of mix, no need to go overboard his first morning, and asked Lois to hand him some bananas.

He must have shocked her into obeying. He hadn't done anything like this in over three years and had wondered if he still had his culinary skills. But he mixed and he poured. When the time came he peeked under the corner of the bubbly pancake, saw the edges looked right, slid the spatula under, and flipped. Lois applauded.

Soon he served up a golden-brown pancake for its taste test. "Get your forks." Just about every man got a fork and dug in. It passed the taste test, and the orders started. He mixed and he poured and he flipped. Workers putting supplies in the pantry and cabinets thought they'd best try some, too, after the accolades came in, even Lois.

It had been impulsive. But fun and the urge to cook began to stir. If he didn't contain it, he could become overwhelmed... before the time was right. But this felt mighty good, as if he'd accomplished the challenge of the day.

All was going well. Jim liked him, didn't probe into his life, and said he could stay here for at least a month, which should be long enough. He was home! And he could renew his acquaintance with a kitchen since he'd pleased Lois, the director's niece.

He felt confident. "So, Lois, you think I could be your assistant?"

"Fine with me. But those decisions are made by the director or his niece. Oh, there's Gloria now."

Thomas looked.

The girl in the shadows he met last night became, as all faces did for him, a study potentially to be replicated on watercolor paper or canvas. His first thought was no. He didn't paint portraits now, he painted characters. Her face was too smoothly pretty, the full lips too smiley, the eyes too blue, re-

flecting the color of her T-shirt, the body lines in the jeans…
whoa! You paint faces, remember!

His scrutiny returned to her face about the time Greg stopped her, wearing a you-made-my-day expression. One might think hers was the same. But Thomas saw deeper than the say-cheese-now kind of smile, and he knew there was another definition of blue besides color.

The woman had a few shadows inside herself. She might, after all, be a subject for his paintbrush.

The moment Gloria stepped into the dining room she saw Greg heading straight for her, which had become a habit of his. He was all smiles. "Glad the meeting went well last night. The Turkey Trot is a great idea."

"So you read the note I left?" He must have, otherwise he wouldn't know about the plans.

"I wanted to thank you in person for sitting in for me."

"No problem. They're very smart and dedicated. Is that… all? I need to get busy here."

He looked like it might *not* be all but said, "You're one dedicated person, Gloria." She saw the admiration in his eyes. "Well, see you later."

She gave a little wave and hastened to the kitchen. Greg had come to the shelter and waited for her, just to say *thank you*? Well, he was a young, single boy. That thought gave her pause. He was only two years younger than she. Chronologically. But she had passed the point of no return to those happy, carefree younger days.

The impact of the adage, *you're only as old as you feel,* had become her own experience. No doubt about it, she was older than Marge.

"I'm running late," she said as if they weren't aware that the men were already eating, some had finished, and several had brought their plates to the counter. Sudie was cleaning one of the stoves. Lon set down a mop and pail. They all spoke.

Lois was tying the top of a trash bag. "You might want some breakfast. We might just have us a new—"

"Already ate," she said, taking a plate that looked like it had been licked clean. She put it into the dishwasher. "Clara had a new recipe to try out this morning. Southern cream biscuits—"

"Southern cream biscuits?" said a voice from the pantry, soon revealed to belong to a bearded man with a ponytail. So Thomas, if she remembered his name right, was a volunteer. She'd never seen him at church, but there could be many reasons for that. She'd never seen Caleb before either because of his deployments in the military.

Thomas walked over and watched her dump the contents of a plate, rinse it, and place it in the dishwasher. "Southern cream biscuits sound almost as good as banana pancakes," he said. Lois giggled. He handed Gloria another plate to contend with. "You must be the niece Jim mentioned."

She glanced at him and back at the plate. "He has more than one niece, so…depends." She didn't like the idea that she'd been discussed, and scrubbed hard at dried egg.

"Depends, huh?"

When he said that, she remembered their exchange last night about that word. She needn't be so touchy. He was a volunteer, and she'd learned quickly volunteers were a special breed of people, kind and caring.

He scoffed. "Jim didn't mention she's impertinent, so…" Catching her quick glance, he added, "Must not be you."

He backed away, and Lois was chuckling.

She knew he was toying with her and turned toward him. "What did Jim say?"

"He said his niece helped with the cooking."

Playing or not, she had to defend herself. "I'm not really a cook."

"Um, that settles it." He nodded. "He *was* talking about you."

Lois was laughing aloud now. He grimaced, but his dark eyes danced. Impulsively, she stuck her hand under the running faucet and flicked the water onto his face.

"At least it wasn't a dish," he said, wiping his beard with both hands as if she'd splashed more than a couple sprinkles.

She wasn't sure what it was about him, but she'd never think of doing that to one of the other workers. Or anyone for that matter. But, if a little thing like that could make him and Lois happy, so be it.

Hearing a chuckle, she looked over and saw Jim standing at the counter. He held up a restraining hand to Gloria. "Now those weren't my exact words, Gloria. I think we have a Joker here, straight out of the comic book."

Thomas held out both hands and reared back. "If we're playing Batman, maybe a Catwoman, too."

"You best remember that," she threatened, reaching for the sprayer and clawing toward him with her other hand.

Jim spoke up. "May be time to get you some clothes, Thomas, and get to that painting."

"Yes sir." Thomas looked around, said thanks to all of them, and walked out, leaving them with the dirty dishes.

Gloria watched them walk out of the kitchen. What kind of volunteer was he? She turned to Lois. "You know him?"

Lois shook her head. "Never saw him before in my life."

Chapter 11

4

Jim led the way out of the dining area and into the hallway. He was quiet, and Thomas wondered if he'd overstepped. There was protocol to observe, like he would do with Jim, an employee with an employer, child with a parent, and numerous other situations. "Hope I wasn't too familiar with the cooking or your niece."

Jim grinned. "I was sitting back watching," he said. "Spiced up the morning a bit. Everybody enjoyed it, and the workers appreciate any help they can get." He stopped at the first door on the right, labeled Clothes Closet. "Gloria didn't seem to mind. It's good to see her having a little fun."

Thomas could understand that. Working in a shelter could be fulfilling but not generally what one called fun. But for him, after spending three years with his companions being homeless men, his home alleys and shelters, and his next meal at the mercy of others, it sure felt good being around women again and being...almost home.

Jim opened the door and switched on the light. Suits and shirts hung along one wall on hangers, with dress shoes on the floor beneath them. Opposite them were folded clothes stacked on shelves. The bottom shelf held a row of what appeared to be new tennis shoes. Farther along were obviously used ones.

They found clothes suitable to paint in, instead of Thomas messing up the holey jeans and T-shirt that hadn't impressed James. When they returned to the kitchen, Thomas saw the ladder and paint waiting. The two stoves were in the middle of the floor; Lon was sweeping where one had sat and another resident was washing grease stains off the opposite wall.

Thomas raised his eyebrows. "I suppose you want it finished before lunch."

"You do that and you can paint the whole town." He chuckled. "I expect soup and sandwiches to be brought in for lunch."

"Soup," Thomas mused, as his grandmother's specialty flashed vividly in his memory. He hadn't meant to say aloud what tripped through his mind. Many times he wondered if he were like Esau who sold his birthright for a bowl of soup, or in his case, a soup recipe.

Jim studied him for a moment then mentioned supper. "An ample supply of salad makings, fruit, and precooked meats will arrive. Some hot food. Like at church homecomings, you know."

"Oh yeah," Thomas said. "Church ladies know how to put out a spread."

Jim gave him another look. "Why don't we get a cup of that coffee and sit over there while these men are finishing up?"

They did, and Jim said, "I'd like to give you a little background on this shelter."

Thomas drank his coffee, just watching the cup most of the time. He could have told Jim the story. The congregation outgrew the little Wildwood Church. The decision to tear it down or not almost split the church until a man donated a lot of money to put it to some good use. Then he fell on hard times not of his own making, and the money stopped coming. Soon after that he had a heart attack.

The ones who wanted to save the little church decided to

honor the man who had given so much of his time through the years to the church and this community. His mother had been a member there all her life.

"I admired the man very much," Jim said, nodding for a moment. Glancing at Jim, Thomas knew the man was struggling to control his emotions. "A picture of him hangs in the church hallway along with those of pastors and others who have contributed in special ways."

There it came, that flood of grief that could wash through Thomas without waiting for an opportune time. He could almost hear his dad singing about the little white church in the wildwood. Feel his loving grandmother's arms around him.

Jim had to know this affected Thomas, but he kept on. "It made the news for a while. The happenings hit us all hard. We knew of the losses that man's boys had. Many times I've seen the older brother at church events. The church he attends sends an annual donation for the shelter. Became an attorney with a good reputation." He paused. "Often thought, where's the younger brother?"

Thomas faced him squarely then, not caring about his own moist eyes. "The younger brother is close to finding out." That brought on a hard emotion, too. "When did you know it was me?"

Jim's bushy gray eyebrows rose slightly. "Maybe it's how you salivated when you said soup."

They both laughed. It could well be.

Jim shook his head. "By itself it wouldn't mean anything. But when you walked in last night I thought there was something familiar about you. Then, watching you, listening to you, it just seemed likely. Then I realized there's definitely a resemblance."

"Beneath all this?" Thomas stroked his beard and shook his ponytail.

"Yes, even if you do look like a hippie."

"Sorry. I think that's before my time." He sighed playfully.

"I was trying to look homeless. Sure didn't think I looked like James."

Jim laughed. "You're doing all right with the homeless part. But, um…I wasn't referring to James."

The earth sort of shook. Thomas supposed he could see other people but not himself. He never thought of looking like his dad.

When his dad lost his money, his heart gave out.

While he still had his sons, his heart still gave out.

Which was more important?

"I think I should tell you something."

Jim said quickly, "You don't need to. Don't have to." He paused. "But I'm here if you want to."

The man on the other side of the table was on the canvas of Thomas's mind and he was eager to paint that into reality. So he told him briefly what he'd been doing and what he hoped to do. Jim listened intently, and Thomas didn't detect any judgment or condemnation from him.

When Thomas finished, Jim said, "I'm going to tell you something I've never told anyone except my Clara." He leaned back for a moment, pondering. "I had a dream. I wanted to be a singer. But I didn't pursue it. Mind you, I can't complain about my life at all. The Lord chose me to serve Him in a special way. I've sung with groups and solo. I've used my voice for the Lord. My life is blessed." He drew a deep breath, and Thomas saw the longing in his eyes. "I wonder what my life might have been if I had. I'll never know." His gaze was sincere. "If I can help you pursue your dream, I want to help."

"You just did. Thank you."

Jim nodded. "And I know this is confidential." He stretched out his arms on the table with the palms of his hands turned up. "Let me pray for you."

He did. And he prayed that Thomas would be blessed in pursuing his dream.

Thomas knew he would know the answer soon, and the thought came with both anticipation and fear.

Chapter 12

With the backpack firmly in place, Thomas walked from Wildwood to the hotel, went around back, and unlocked the door. He stepped out of the bright sunlight into a darkened, stuffy hallway. The air was stale. He went to the kitchen doorway and remembered his grandmother, singing her hymns and laughing and cooking and making everyone happy.

Across the hall was the dining room, its drapes tightly closed. In the dimness he could make out the room filled with round tables and vacant chairs that could easily seat 300 people. The sights and sounds and smells penetrated his memory like a sweet song, yet also a lament of how what one takes for granted can vanish.

He didn't remember the drapes ever being closed before except the day he left over three years ago. At any time he could look out the windows and see the trees and shrubs and gardens. The hotel sat back from the road, on the incline, as if saying it wouldn't crowd the streets since it wasn't really a part of those residences and office buildings but a separate, comforting place, a place of refuge. It had been that to him, when his family was alive. Now they were only memories in his mind and in his heart. Only the dull sound of his footsteps sounded along the carpeted hallway.

The living room was better illuminated from the sun pressing against the curtains as if wanting desperately to enter. Looking around, he smiled at the cozy room with its seating arrangements that could delight a small group or be arranged for a large group. The piano his mother had played while the family sang sat idle in a corner.

He walked through the room and opened the glass doors. The foyer was brightly lighted by sunshine streaming through the glass panels on the upper part of the front door. Near the wall opposite the door sat the large desk where guests could come in and register. The idle computer sat, along with the lamp and telephone, waiting. The staircase was waiting, too, but Thomas looked past it.

Across from the living room was his dad's office. After Thomas's mom died, his dad cut back on his hours in the law office. He liked to hear the happy voices of people in the hotel, getting to know each other, sitting before the fire in the living room during the winter, feeling like family and being close to his mother since James and Thomas were away at school much of the time, traveling, or just doing their own things.

Thomas's dad said he'd spent too much time making money, investing, selling off larger hotels in the chain his own dad had left him. He wanted to make this like the family place that it should have been when his wife was living, instead of holing up in the big roomy house where James now lived. His ambition became to leave his sons a legacy, enough wealth so each would have time to be a family man, not a moneymaker.

But then…his dad's heart gave out when his money did. His investments had been wise. The companies he'd invested with had not been. When the banks failed, when the investment companies went bankrupt, his purpose had died. His purpose had not been his sons but his money. And it had failed him.

Next to his dad's office was his grandmother's bedroom. The hotel had been her life. She wasn't about to live with Thomas's dad in the big house. Her joy was her church and the kitchen and her grandsons. She'd said Thomas's dad could be the executive. She'd be the chief cook, and she'd been the best.

Thomas took a deep breath and touched the polished wooden railing bordering the elegant staircase, his gaze captured by the crystal chandelier hanging from three stories high. He moved slowly up the steps toward the suite, where no inviting food smells greeted him as they once did, just dry, stuffy air like something closed up for a long time.

He had no need to explore any rooms on the second floor but climbed on up to the third. He hadn't locked the inside doors when he'd left. If anyone broke in they wouldn't have needed to break down any door other than the front or back.

The third floor consisted of only the suite and the two rooms that had been converted into his studio while he was still in college. He opened the door to the suite first. The sitting room was cozy with a fireplace and a bay window where one might sit and look down upon the beautiful pink-blossomed cherry trees on the green front lawn in spring or the lush foliage in summer, the changing leaves in fall or the blanket of snow in winter.

Light filtered through the soft white curtains in the bedroom. It was a beautifully decorated room with a king-sized bed. He'd slept there many times. In fact, he'd slept in every room. He'd loved the sleepovers with his grandmother when he was a boy and could sleep in any vacant room he wished or even in the room with her.

As he grew older however, his real home had been his studio. His heart quickened at the thought of going inside, and that's why he saved it for last, although his first impulse had been to run up the stairs and see if it was still there.

Of course it was. He stepped inside and opened the blinds, ones that could be adjusted so he could use the right light for his paintings. The view was like the one in the suite's sitting room: the front lawn and tops of cherry trees. Turning around to survey the room he almost laughed. There were no easels out, except one big one too tall for the closet; no paints; no spills, empty coffee cups, trash cans running over, or canvases. It looked like someone's abandoned room, not a studio. Supplies were packed away in the closets.

Two long tables were situated against a wall where he could lay out sketches or frame paintings. A couple artist's chairs and a stool sat idle at the tables. Off to the side wall was the twin bed. Next to it was the bathroom. He hadn't wanted to stay in a dorm when in college but wanted to live in this room, and when he didn't have to study, he'd sketch and paint. He thought he could live in this room forever, it had all he needed—his art materials and a place to sleep.

But that's when he had family downstairs and across town. Family and friends.

Now, with his family gone except James, he felt the emptiness and loneliness of an empty hotel. He thought of James's family. But he couldn't allow any envy or hope or thoughts about romantic possibilities. He'd made a commitment. He would see it through.

He had his memories, his purpose, his Lord. Yet for some strange reason, he had a yearning for something else, a love of his own. But that would have to wait until he'd finished his project. He was on the home stretch. Those yearnings must wait a little longer.

He'd almost lost his life at times but had found his soul. Jesus said something like that; you have to lose your life to find it. Of course *He'd* meant spiritually. But the spiritual applied to all areas of life; it wasn't separate.

Shrugging out of the backpack, he laid it on a table, pulled out a chair, and started to unfasten the bag. Instead, his arms stretched out on the table, he bent and laid his head down, and the tears came.

His tears were a prayer. He couldn't form the words because they were about his entire life. The blessings, the losses, the grief, the wonderful memories, his past, his present, his wandering, and his wondering what he was doing now. And for now having returned for the ending of the commitment he'd made to God.

Finally, when he raised his head, he felt the peace that only the Lord could bring, felt the joy of life and possibilities and challenge. With it remained the uncertainty of how his three-year commitment would end. He was still just a human being who had a purpose in what he'd done, and his heart's desire was that it be worthwhile from the human standpoint. But he couldn't know the ending of what he'd planned, just as his dad hadn't known his ending.

He had to think about the practical side of things. He'd contact his agent, Frank, and see if he had any royalties from the reproductions that sold in the area to tourists.

Thinking of Frank, he remembered his last conversation with him. Thomas had thought he had a ready-made career when James married Arlene and her dad was a well-known agent for writers and artists. Frank had looked at his paintings right there in Thomas's studio. "Reminds me of Jules's work," he'd said, referring to a top-selling client.

Elation swept through Thomas. At the time, he'd just returned from France after spending a summer there learning his art, visiting the galleries, and painting scenes of Paris, looking at Mona Lisa's smile, even—

"You can't mean it compares to Jules's paintings," Thomas said, although he thought his not only compared but exceeded; but he could possibly be biased.

"Yes," Frank said.

"Then you'll represent me, try to get an exhibit?"

Frank was already shaking his head. "I have Jules. We've worked on his career. You don't expect me to drop—"

"No," Thomas said and scoffed. "Of course not. I know you must have many clients."

"Oh yes, but tell you what. I can't do anything with the Paris pictures."

Thomas felt his heart drop. Those were the ones in which he'd put the most time and hope.

"But I can see about having reproductions made of the DC pictures. Those should sell to tourists."

Well, it was a start, so Thomas signed a contract. At least he had an agent.

Frank looked at him like a businessman not a relative. "You have anything else?"

"I've done portraits."

Frank's eyes bore into his. "Portraits?"

He was making Thomas feel uncomfortable. "I guess there's not a great market for portraits."

Frank shrugged a shoulder. "I might be able to get work for you occasionally. It's a chance. Mention you while playing golf and ask if anybody wants their wife painted. Contact some businesses and see if any CEOs want a portrait."

"You're making fun of me."

"No. I'm being honest. I could do that. I'd think the assignments would be few and far between though."

"Yeah, I agree."

Frank walked to the window and turned his back on Thomas. After a while he turned. "You're good, Thomas. As good as thousands of other artists out there. So, since you say you prefer portraits, why don't you paint people?"

Portraits are *people.* "People?"

"Paint people who have a special meaning to you. These," he said, gesturing to the ones in the dining room that Frank said tourists would like, "are what's out there." He'd pointed out the window. "Paint what's in here." He'd patted his heart.

Frank left that day leaving Thomas feeling like a failure. He'd already painted his mom and dad. People? What kind of people did he care about? The elderly like his grandmother, whose every line in her face was dear to him? Would that mean anything to anyone else?

He couldn't force the creativity, couldn't conjure up some passion. He had had none.

But that had changed. And it wasn't finished yet, so he needed to get the studio set up and the supplies he needed. This was a three-year pass or fail course.

He couldn't stop before getting the final grade.

Chapter 13

Each morning, Gloria passed the dining room, heard Thomas's voice, and from the doorway glimpsed him in the kitchen. She walked on by, went into Jim's office, and turned on the computer at her desk. She didn't know what to think about Thomas. Or herself, for that matter. Her sprinkling water on him and his referring to her as Catwoman seemed inappropriate after she asked Jim about him and learned Thomas was taking Caleb's bed for now. So he was homeless and not a volunteer.

Later that morning he stepped inside the office and said he hoped he hadn't offended her by taking over the cooking that morning. She politely told him no, and looked hard at a form on her desk as if she were very busy. If he'd been a volunteer she would have joked and said she wasn't much of a cook anyway. Jim said they're just people, and she knew that, but she didn't think she should be too friendly with a homeless man.

One of the residents stuck his head in the door later and said, "Just wanted you to know I liked my eggs hard cooked." Jim was there, and they had trouble holding back their laughter until he had time to get far enough away not to hear them.

In the following days however, she discovered Thomas did

a good job painting the kitchen. And although living there like a homeless man, he volunteered for just about everything, and Jim allowed it. He took over cooking breakfast and came up with a surprise every Wednesday morning, saying it was the middle of the week and he didn't want anyone to get bored. *He* certainly wasn't boring. When Thomas popped in to prepare a special supper once a week they applauded and whistled.

Lois gladly became his assistant. Gloria wondered if he was trying to take over Lois's job. But in the weeks that followed, nothing came across her desk to indicate Jim was paying him.

She was relieved to be out of the kitchen but felt less needed than ever. Now that spring was turning into summer, the flowers and vegetable gardens were thriving, and she had more time to tend to her and Clara's flower beds in the backyard. Clara had admonished in a Bible study, "Bloom where you're planted." At least the flowers obeyed, so she often adorned the dining room tables with fresh ones. Amazing how much the men appreciated such little effort. They'd stop by her office and tell her.

Anything a person did for the shelter was worthwhile, and she liked the feeling of being helpful. She liked the men, the workers—loved Clara and Jim—even liked…how Thomas livened up the place, kind of like the flowers.

She rather regretted not joking with him like the others did, but no way could she encourage any false impression in a homeless man. And who knew what his problem might be? Curious, she said suddenly, "Jim, doesn't Thomas have to fill out an application?"

"No. He's temporary in case Caleb returns."

She didn't question that because Jim was the director, but she'd been under the impression they closely documented everything and everyone. She thought he might have lost his job and hadn't found another. But he didn't leave in the mornings like the men looking for work, although he was gone in the afternoons. After she noticed him sitting in on classes taking notes, she asked Jim, "Does Thomas have some kind of condition I need to be aware of?"

"No worry. But his condition"—Jim chuckled—"is confidential."

So…he was temporary and confidential.

That description brought Raymond to mind. His *confidential* with someone else is what led to her and Raymond being temporary instead of permanent.

Focusing on the computer screen and glancing at the time in the corner, she realized she hadn't accomplished a lick of work in thirty minutes. Why was she thinking about him anyway? Certainly didn't have anything to do with that infamous state of being she'd heard about. If she were on the rebound she'd turn to Greg who had his life in order and made clear his availability. But she always did like trying to figure out the mystery in a book.

She decided she'd never figure Thomas's puzzle out the day Jim entered the office and walked near her desk to report, "Caleb's month is up. The doctors approved his return, so he'll be here in the morning."

Gloria pondered that a moment. When Heather and Bobby had joined her, Jim, and Clara for lunch after church one Sunday so Clara and Heather could discuss Bible school, Heather tearfully vowed she wouldn't live the kind of life her mom had with her alcoholic dad. She'd lived without Caleb while he served in the military and could again if needed for her and Bobby's welfare.

"So Heather's not taking him back?"

"Caleb will be in therapy and on medication for a while. The doctors don't think he has an addiction, but he used alcohol to get relief from his pain." He sighed sadly. "Just caused more pain. But"—he perked up—"there's a chance that family can be together again."

A thought seared her brain. "Does Thomas leaving mean I'll go back to cooking?"

"No, no," he said. "You're needed to help with the job fair. The church wants to know if we can take on some additional responsibilities. You know they have representatives coming from all over."

She knew quite well, since Jim was on the church committee for the job fair and this was an annual event geared especially for the many homeless in DC and surrounding areas. The church secretary already carried a full load. Gloria had helped with correspondence to and from representatives coming from DC, Maryland, Virginia, and some as far away as Tennessee and Georgia.

"The need this year has exceeded all expectations," Jim said with his eyebrows almost a straight line. "In past years we've had an abundance of homeless and unemployed. This year it's record high." He shook his head. "Some of our own church members are hurting. Not homeless but threatened with foreclosures."

His words gave her a shot of reality. Comparatively she had nothing to complain about. But she didn't even have a house that could be foreclosed. And no family to support either. Assisting with the fair, maybe she wouldn't feel so much like a piece of furniture good for decoration only. "What can I do?"

"Help our residents who're able to work and our own church members with résumés. Maybe give some instruction on being interviewed. Many who haven't been able to get work are desperate and scared. Like Caleb."

During Jim's moment of reflection he turned and walked over to sit at his desk. He looked across at her. "This is right up your alley, since you managed a bookstore and have some knowledge of interviewing and résumés."

"I can help with résumés, thanks to my friend here." She patted her computer. "But how to be interviewed is a different matter. I hired workers, mostly summer and holiday help, but that was similar to the way I was hired. Another worker knew me. My résumé was being a college student needing a summer job. That extended to holidays. Then the job became permanent after I graduated." She didn't bother to mention the district manager had taken a liking to her and recommended promotions. "I don't know, Uncle Jim. I've failed to find a job for supporting myself."

"You have it up here." He pointed at his head. "But I wouldn't expect you to take all this on by yourself. I have a very capable volunteer—"

Volunteer?

At that moment he walked into the office, his brown eyes dancing as if he'd just enjoyed having water sprinkled on his beard.

Amazing what could happen from one moment to the next.

Jim's request promoted her to the challenge of helping the church secretary with this huge project.

Thomas's presence demoted her confidence down to reality. She had a strong suspicion she was going to be like Lois, an assistant to a homeless man.

Chapter 14 3

Thomas had stopped in the hallway rather than walking in and interrupting Jim and Gloria's conversation. He considered retracing his steps but realized Jim was explaining the job fair work to be done.

Jim had explained it to him at breakfast. Clara came with Jim, and the three of them ate breakfast together after the men had been fed and went about their activities of job hunting, attending classes, doing yard work, tending to their personal needs the best they could, or for one man, biding time while hoping the natural healing process would take place.

Thomas had been under the impression Clara was incapacitated but saw that although she wore a shoe boot she otherwise seemed perfectly functional. "Jim told me you'd be making the Southern cream biscuits this morning," she said, a playfulness about her like he'd seen in Jim and had seen once in Gloria. "I'm jealous and have to find out if they're tasty as mine." She huffed and sat at the table. "Jim says you're making everybody fat."

"Fat's not my expertise if I can help it." He held up his hands. "But this was your recipe, so don't blame me."

He served their plates and, at their request, sat down with

them. While Clara ate, Lois came over and sat for a while, asking about Clara's foot and when she was coming back.

"I'm not," Clara said and then smiled at Thomas, using his words. "If I can help it. I've been spoiled since Gloria came to us. I've slowed down with this contraption on my foot, but I can still do everything at home. The work here is for younger people like Gloria and Thomas."

"Is Gloria going to stay?" Lois asked.

"No longer than she has to," Clara said. They all looked sad at that.

Thomas wondered at the remark about Gloria. Maybe she'd been in an accident and was still recuperating.

Lois touched the petal of a wilting flower. "Has she come in yet? I can fix her a plate."

"She ate cereal," Jim said, "then went out to cut some fresh flowers."

Thomas supposed she'd rather have cereal than find out how his Southern cream biscuits tasted.

"I'll go ahead and take the wilted ones out of the vases," Lois said. "But I have to know what you think of Thomas's biscuits."

Clara looked down at her empty plate and sighed. "It's a little soon to tell," she said reflectively. "The red-eye gravy may have changed the taste. I might have to try another. So, if there are any left, I'll just take one home for my lunch."

Ah, of the three women around here he'd like please, this might be two down, one to go. But he warned himself against that kind of thinking. He had a mission, he had a goal, and he wasn't letting James and his family interfere with that. He certainly couldn't give in to the temptation of female companionship. Not that he'd been given the opportunity.

Lois left the table to empty the vases. Clara asked Jim how Gloria was getting along with the job fair. She addressed Thomas then. "That was always the most difficult for me," she said. "So many details, and technology isn't my forte."

Jim explained the additional workload. "Gloria and I might be working a few late hours."

Clara said she understood and patted Jim's hand. Her kind eyes, in a pleasant face, looked across at Thomas with acceptance. "Thanks for what you're doing here, Thomas. And"—she paused a moment before saying—"welcome."

He had a feeling she knew who he was. His confidential conversation with Jim had applied to his purpose not to keep secret Thomas's identity from his wife. She had every right to know who replaced her and Gloria in the kitchen and stayed in the shelter to which she devoted so much of her life.

"I need to tell you," Jim said after Clara left to get her biscuit. "Caleb will be released in the morning. Can you pick him up in the truck and bring him here?"

"Certainly," Thomas said. Anything he could do for Jim or the shelter, he would. He'd borrowed the truck to drive to James's office for his packages and made a trip to Frank's office for the small royalty checks he made from reproductions. Frank didn't ask any questions, but being the dad of James's wife, he would have been told that Thomas had been wandering around the country and was living in a shelter.

They probably thought he was a lost soul, not knowing his wandering was how he found his soul.

Now that Caleb would be returning, Thomas's routine would change. Since he wouldn't be spending nights at the shelter, he would need more than afternoon light and water. He'd need to get the electricity turned on.

He would make that call. And, too, he may not have time in the morning to clean his side of the room that he shared with Sam, so he'd get that done today and take his few personal items from the bathroom. "I'll go up and take the sheets off the bed and get them into the washer."

"You have a place to stay tonight?"

"Only a choice of a dozen or so empty rooms."

Jim smiled knowingly. "The hotel."

Thomas nodded. "That's where I've been in the afternoons. Oh," he added, "I'd like to help with the job fair if you can use me."

Jim looked pleased. "Get the laundry underway and come to my office."

That's what led to his standing in the hallway listening to the conversation between Jim and Gloria, after he'd set the sheets to washing.

What surprised him was Gloria's saying, "I've failed to find a job for myself."

What did that mean? She's not pleased working here? Is that the reason for the hint of sadness he detected in her?

Maybe God's landing a job fair in their laps wasn't just for Thomas's benefit but Gloria's. And he was the volunteer Jim mentioned to her.

So he walked into their office.

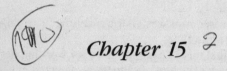

Chapter 15 2

"Pull up a chair, Thomas," Jim said. "I was telling Gloria you might help with the job fair."

He unfolded the padded chair propped against the wall and set it in a spot between their desks, so he could easily talk to both. "How can I help you?" he asked Gloria.

"You could tell me…" She paused, as if reluctant to ask. "What are your skills?"

Hoping to lighten the tension, he quipped, "Well, I'm a kitchen painter." Jim chuckled and shook his head like Thomas might be hopeless. Gloria's glance seemed to reveal no doubt of that. He cleared his throat. "Jim mentioned interviewing. I have a little experience along that line. And I remember how job fairs were handled in college." He didn't want to say he also remembered what his dad taught him about it.

"I didn't attend those. I already had a job I liked," she said. Her gaze moved to the computer. He wondered if she were surprised a homeless man was educated. Many were. He'd met a professor, with a PhD, in a shelter because of an accusation, later proved false, that put him out of his job and home. Illness without enough insurance to pay the bills, a factory closing unexpectedly, or an investment firm going bankrupt could do it. Or…losing a job unexpectedly.

She glanced his way again. "I would start with résumés."

He nodded. "Get a résumé form and we'll go from there. Oh, but I'm not available in the afternoons. Not tomorrow morning either."

"This morning?"

"Sorry."

"At your convenience," she said politely, but he detected the edge in her tone. Jim looked amused.

Thomas stood and folded the chair. Standing close to her desk he noticed the sun had highlighted her light brown hair with a hint of reddish-gold. She looked up and pushed her errant wavy lock behind her ear. He strongly suspected those eyes, more gray than blue today and holding a hint of uncertainty, should be replicated. But he'd need to know what lay behind the expression before he could paint it.

Returning thoughts to her now questioning gaze, he quickly explained. "This morning I need to get my room ready and clean the bathroom since Caleb returns in the morning."

She drew in a sharp breath and looked past him. "Jim, Heather thinks she and Bobby should be at the rehab center to show her support when Caleb's released. But she wants someone else to be with them in case Caleb demands to go home with them. I know she'll call and ask me." She spoke hesitantly. "I want to be supportive of her, but I don't want to be in the middle of a family squabble."

"I don't want that either," Jim said as Thomas returned his chair to the wall. "The rehab center is releasing Caleb into our custody, so someone from here needs to pick him up. I already asked Thomas. Guess I won't need you to do that, Thomas."

Thomas turned to face him. "I'll be glad to go along. Caleb's probably embarrassed and needs to know he has friends here. And I can thank him for his bed."

"Sounds like a plan," Jim said. "You'll need the car."

"My little economy car is small," Gloria reminded Jim.

Jim nodded. "Mine's bigger. And I appreciate this. I want to be here in the morning when the produce arrives from the community farm."

Thomas would like to be here for that, too, but he could look at food another time. This would be an ideal time to interview the way his dad taught him. He'd interview Gloria, Heather, and Caleb by listening. Just as they would not ask Caleb about life in a rehab center, they wouldn't ask what life had been like for a homeless man.

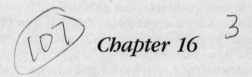

Chapter 16

People could reveal a lot about themselves in what they might think was only casual conversation. And that group was trying to be casual. Caleb and Bobby related on the child's level. Thomas watched the traffic and the reflection of women and boy in the rearview mirror, and he managed to let Caleb know the men were looking forward to his return, especially Sam.

Caleb said he'd be in therapy for a while and on medication. He now understood he had an illness that could be cured. Heather had been a cosmetologist until Bobby was born. They'd managed in the one-bedroom apartment until Caleb was discharged from the military. Bobby wasn't in school yet, she had no one to watch him, so she couldn't try to get a job. She left unspoken what they all knew. She wouldn't allow the troubled Caleb to be alone with their son.

Thomas wasn't surprised to hear Gloria saying she had a degree in business management, considering her expertise when helping Jim in his office, her work with classroom schedules, and her being asked to help the church in an even greater capacity with the job fair. He'd overheard she had managed a bookstore. In the car he learned that a store she managed had been with Walkway Christian Stores, which he knew to be a major chain with several stores in and around DC. He'd seen them in malls.

Heather apparently already knew Gloria's parents were missionaries in Ecuador and asked about them. Gloria had attended a university in DC to be close to Clara and Jim for holidays and visits. She'd worked in a DC store and moved to the Shenandoah Mountains where she was promoted to manager and shared an apartment with a girlfriend.

"I plan to be interviewed at the job fair," Heather said. "Some church people have offered to help with Bobby. In a few weeks he'll be in kindergarten."

"Maybe somebody at the job fair will give me a job," Caleb said. "I'll be glad to do anything."

When Heather asked Gloria if she was going to be interviewed, Gloria said she would like to but then hesitated. "But I don't want to take time or a job away from any others. My position in this is to help the others, not myself."

Thomas thought it time he spoke about that. "Gloria, it wouldn't be wrong to have a couple interviews of your own. If someone else were more qualified than you, they'd get the job anyway."

He saw her eyes brighten for a moment. "I suppose that's right." In the rearview mirror, he watched her and Heather smile at each other. "I'll think about it," she said.

When they dropped Heather and Bobby off at their apartment, Bobby begged his dad to stay, and Caleb explained he was sick right now and needed to be at the shelter. Bobby finally accepted that he could visit his dad there. With that settled, Thomas returned to the center with Gloria and Caleb. Caleb headed to Jim's office to report in.

Thomas knew Gloria could joke with the workers and volunteers, and she could be spontaneous, loving toward Jim, caring and helpful with the men, friendly with Heather and Bobby, and conscientious with her job. She was the kind of person anyone would want to be around and quite attractive to look at. She had sparked his curiosity. With him, he thought she was not indifferent. Just…wary. Rightfully so. She didn't know a lot about him. And if she did, she might be even more wary.

The following morning after breakfast he went into the office. Jim said he needed to speak to the RA and had a few other things to do, so Thomas and Gloria could have the office to themselves for a while.

Gloria showed Thomas a couple résumé forms.

"Both these are fine," he said "But let's try this one. You go ahead and fill it out."

"Me? But I'm not going to be interviewed. Why don't we have Sam or one of the other men do this?"

"Because," he said, "you'll be preparing Sam or one of the others to have some idea what to expect in the interview. My job is to"—he decided not to use the word *teach*—"to suggest to you what you might suggest to them."

She actually laughed. "You're being very careful with me, aren't you?"

"Very," he said, breathing a sigh of relief. Maybe she didn't really enjoy being so…careful…around him.

She began to fill out the résumé. He walked over to the window and looked out. Maybe he had attended Sunday school in this room as a boy. And his dad when he was a boy, too. His grandmother could have taught in it. His gaze moved to outside the window. A resident was cutting the grass with a push mower. Another was emptying the trash into the bins, partially obscured by shrubs at the end of the side road. There were many jobs the homeless could do if given the chance, options for people such as Caleb who declared, "I'll do anything."

He watched a man emptying the trash. A piece of paper fell onto the ground and was blown by the wind. The man hurried after it. When something apparently got caught in the lid, he opened the lid and pushed it down.

A man with the mower backed up to try again at a stubborn weed. It didn't cut, so he pulled it. This was what his dad taught him to watch for. Take a landscaper out to see the area to be worked. His reaction would tell you what kind of worker he'd be without your asking a question.

Thomas's grandmother chose a different method. "Cook me a meal," she'd say, and that's how she judged a cook for the hotel.

He couldn't do that with the ones coming to the job fair who would be interviewed in the church basement. But just listening told you a lot.

He turned when Gloria said, "Finished."

$$\frac{\begin{array}{r} 192 \\ 89 \end{array}}{103}$$

Chapter 17 4

Gloria handed the résumé to Thomas. While filling it out she thought about his saying that if others were more qualified than she they'd get the job. She would print copies of her own résumé and give them to some of the reps but not take up personal interview time. She'd already applied at bookstores with no results. Now it was time to try for employment with other businesses. Prospective employers would be right here at the church instead of her having to traipse all over DC to meet them.

And, too, she was being ridiculous with that attitude about Thomas. He seemed to like…everyone, and he hadn't given her any reason, as Greg had, to be distant with him. No, her reticence around him had to be because she'd been badly burned and didn't want to chance anything. But he hadn't given any indication he wanted to pursue her. Nope.

That bearded, pony-tailed fellow, looking like a lean athlete in worn jeans, set the folding chair in front of Jim's desk. As if he were an employer, he sat in Jim's chair. "Please have a seat, Miss Seely."

The situation was really so ridiculous, she laughed. His

eyes danced for a moment, and then he cleared his throat and perused the résumé as if serious.

She expected him to say what she'd heard numerous times and ask why she left her job, and she would say personal reasons. But he surprised her by saying, "Are you working anywhere now, Miss Seely?"

"A homeless shelter."

"I don't see it listed here."

"It doesn't count."

"Why not?"

"It's a charity place not a business. It wouldn't be an impressive part of my experience."

"It impresses me," Thomas said seriously.

She stared. Felt warm. Why would she want to impress him? What difference did it make? He was a homeless man. Anyone who has any kind of job probably impresses a person without one.

And…why was she letting a homeless man interview her, even if this was just pretending?

She'd lost her man, her job, her apartment, most of her savings, and now she was losing her senses! Slightly miffed, she said, "Are you going to put on your résumé that you worked as an executive, interviewing people for placement in jobs?"

He lowered his eyes to the desk and the paper in front of him. She'd meant that to be clever or amusing, but it sounded so…condescending.

Did he feel embarrassed or intimidated?

Maybe he was trying to think of something to say, as was she. He was the first to speak. "You're working as an assistant to the director of this center, and I assume getting paid for it. As part of your job, you'll be assisting others in preparing for interviews. This wouldn't count for me, but it would for you."

She felt like a heel. "I'm sorry," she whispered. She knew, and had even been told, that staff and volunteers never talk down to a homeless person or one of the residents. And of course one shouldn't do it to anyone, anyway.

"For what?" he asked seriously.

"I…offended you."

Thomas scoffed. "That sounds like a politically correct kind of word." He shook his head. "I can take the truth. Sometimes we need others to, um, put us in our place, so to speak."

She closed her eyes for a moment. To what place had she relegated him? The place of a homeless and jobless man? But wasn't that exactly what he was?

"I'm just—" She started to stand. "I'm not cut out for this."

"No," he said. "That was perfect."

Stunned, she kept sitting there.

"What a really good interviewer does is find a touchy spot in the one applying for the job. Find the vulnerability. Don't ask the expected questions. That's the main thing you need to tell those coming to be prepared. They will already have the right information and recommendations on their résumé. The employer wants to know what makes them tick. Prepare the interviewee for the unexpected."

"Fortunately," she admitted, "you're not a real employer or you would have summarily dismissed me right away."

He seemed to think that was as funny as having water thrown on his beard. However, she did learn a valuable lesson about herself and what she could tell others.

"Just a little more," he said.

She nodded. Maybe he had some more little tricks up his T-shirt sleeve.

"All right," he began. "You didn't include a recommendation letter with your résumé. I assume you can get—"

"Oh, believe me. Mine is a model recommendation letter."

She regretted the way she said that, but only an eyebrow lifted a fraction. He went on to his next question. "The Walkway stores are nationwide. Would you be willing to relocate?"

"No." She'd starve before she'd work for that chain. Oh

boy, she was learning lessons. About herself. She could honestly say, "Clara and Jim are my only relatives, except a sister in another state, and she's busy with family." She figured he'd heard the conversations in the car. "My parents come here on furlough."

"Would you consider working anywhere other than a bookstore?"

"I have no other experience."

"Sure you do," he contradicted. "Despite your opinion of it, your working here qualifies you to at least do desk or clerical work at a bed-and-breakfast, hotel, motel, resort, conference center. Would that kind of work be too menial?"

Her mouth dropped open. Had she given the impression she thought working here was menial? "No. No kind of work is too menial. But I doubt I'd make any more money at those places than here. I have education and experience. And I need to support myself instead of Jim and Clara doing it."

Oh dear. She'd done it again. He was living in a homeless shelter and being supported by charity.

She stood and folded the chair. "Thank you. I've learned a lot." About herself, that is. She leaned the chair against the wall and returned to the chair behind her desk. He still sat at Jim's desk, watching her. "I know I have sounded cynical," she said. "That's because I am, and not because of anything you said or did."

He looked at her kindly as if he were Jim sitting there. She felt inclined to go a little further. "Maybe I'm not ready to apply for a job just yet."

"I agree," he said. "I recommend you stay right where you are for the time being."

"Well," she said, feeling embarrassed, "you just helped one unemployed person know how to lose a job."

Trying to control her tongue, she clicked into her e-mails and found one from the church. She saw him get up and move her way, but she gazed at the computer. "The church secretary sent the list of members who will attend the interview preparation meeting."

He stood over her computer. "Gloria."

She mustn't let an unemployed man unnerve her. After all, *she* was making only minimum wage. Her education and experience wasn't doing much for *her*. She forced her gaze to his eyes.

"You have finer qualities than you know. I'd hire you in a moment."

That just made things worse. For some strange reason she couldn't look away from his serious brown eyes. She wished he'd laugh or something. But he didn't. He just said seriously. "See you in the morning."

As he walked out she watched his confident stride and well-groomed ponytail. What would he hire her for? To groom his ponytail? She couldn't even keep her own in place. She shoved her wisp of hair away from her face with a little more force than she'd intended.

She'd tried to joke with herself, hoping she'd laugh.

She didn't.

Chapter 18 3

Keeping her mind on her job, Gloria sent a copy of the résumé form to the church secretary to send to all the unemployed members along with a schedule for those wanting instruction on being interviewed. She would take the six females, and Thomas would have the seven males.

By lunchtime she felt like she'd accomplished more in a couple hours than she normally did during an entire day. But she'd been determined to think about nothing but work. She called to tell Clara she would come home for lunch instead of eating at the shelter.

She'd planned to have a pleasant conversation about their respective mornings but by the time she arrived in Clara's kitchen, the guilt had returned. "The questions he asked about the bookstore, why I left, just brought all the emotional baggage to the surface, Aunt Clara. I understand that, but I was rude to him. And condescending. He's helpful in many ways at the center, and he's helping me. But…he's homeless, and I should be helping him."

Clara set sandwiches on the table. "Honey, a lot of the homeless help others. At the center, mowing the grass for us and some of the neighbors. Some have jobs. When the pipes get stopped up, Sam is the one we call on."

"I know. I guess having to think about what I want to *forget* about just upset me. And I said things to Thomas that I shouldn't when he's just trying to help."

"Remember the day that red light came on in your car and one of the men checked it out and said you were low on oil? Did that upset you?"

"Of course not. I appreciated it."

Clara nodded. "Do you say condescending things to the other residents?"

The line of this questioning made Gloria feel she might lose this job, too, no matter how much Clara and Jim loved her. "No," she said honestly. "I would never do that." She sighed, trying to make sense of it to herself. "Thomas seems different. It's like…we all need him instead of him needing us."

Clara's eyebrows lifted, and she bit into her sandwich. Gloria felt the need to try to explain. "Really, Aunt Clara, I've never been rude to any of the residents, or the volunteers or workers. I'm sorry."

Clara nodded as she chewed then swallowed. "Honey, Jim has told us both, probably me more than you, how kind and sweet you are. The residents and the volunteers all love you."

Hot tears smarted in Gloria's eyes. Before she could find the right words to say, Clara spoke again. "Think about it. Maybe you can answer why you react to him that way."

Gloria felt warm under Clara's studied scrutiny. But she needed help. And she didn't want to be around the residents if she was a hindrance. She wouldn't want to diminish Thomas's confidence.

Gloria sighed. "It's just my insecurity acting up. He's content with where he is. And I'm fearful. I should be the one who's content and helping him. It's…unsettling."

Clara nodded, lifted her mug, and eyed Gloria over the top of it. "That might be it. Or…"

"Or? What?" Gloria held her emotional breath.

Clara returned her mug to the table. "Jim talks to Thomas like he's a son. He would never say things to the other residents that he does to Thomas. You've heard those two go at it. Thomas is more like family. Or a friend." Clara paused. "You've told me that occasionally a resident has spoken harshly, if not directly to you, around you."

"Well yes, but I knew it wasn't directed at me. It's their situation or emotional state or even mental condition. None of us take it personally."

As soon as she said that word her eyes locked with Clara's. Slowly Clara lowered her gaze to her cup and traced a finger around the rim, silent, making Gloria feel the impact of her words as if they were a hyena tripping over her mind, laughing.

Personally?

She was taking Thomas personally?

"Well," Gloria said quickly. "I will not take him personally. He's a homeless man like the rest of the residents. Just because he acts superior doesn't mean he is. It's just my sense of inferiority acting up." She stood. "Thanks for the advice."

"I really didn't give you any. You came up with your own conclusions." Clara grinned.

Gloria exhaled heavily. "That's what psychiatrists do, isn't it? Make the patients answer their own questions?"

Clara's eyes met hers, and her eyebrows lifted slightly.

Gloria closed her eyes for a moment. "Like you've told me so many times, I just need to stop feeling rejected, dejected, down on myself." She held up her hands. "Okay, I'm done with that. Thanks for lunch. I'd better be getting back."

On the way back she thought about that again. She wasn't taking Thomas personally. She'd heard of strange attractions happening when a person had been hurt or jilted and turned to another on the rebound. But she hadn't turned to anybody.

And if she were on the rebound she'd settle for Greg, who was secure in his job and made it clear he was available.

Clara and Jim and she had talked about this being an emotional time for her and that it would take time to heal. That's what it was.

No way would she even consider taking a mysterious, volunteer, homeless, unemployed man…personally.

$$\frac{192}{\quad 97\quad}$$
$$95$$

Chapter 19

Thomas jogged and walked the ten miles from Wildwood to the hotel. Soon after he went inside and raced up the stairs he took his personal items from his backpack and put them in the studio bathroom. While he was taking his sketch pad out, he saw the electric company vehicle turn into the driveway, and he hurried to the front door.

After the electricity was on and everything checked out, he went into the living room where he'd left the lamps on. It was a room cozy enough to enjoy alone. Now that he'd be staying in the hotel at night he might sit in there in the evenings, take a little time off from sketching and painting, lounge in an easy chair, and read a book by the light of a lamp on an end table

He thought of how easily one could take for granted what seemed like a simple activity. But after being on the streets so long, and in shelters, he knew even the simplest of things were luxuries. Now that he would no longer be staying at the center, he would eat his evening meals here, except for the one night of the week he'd continue cooking for the residents

Now that most of his sketching was finished, he'd try to have his work done before Christmas. When he'd taken a course in pastels, the instructor said to put the bones in first

They wouldn't show after you get the flesh on, but without the bones the painting would be flat and lifeless, just like the human body couldn't stand without the skeleton.

The bones were his sketches. By the end of the year he should know if all he had were skeletons, or if his paintings were not only flesh and blood but spirit and soul. In the studio he took out the paintings of the first homeless man and first volunteer he'd painted. He set them on easels, and if they never came alive for anyone else, they did for him.

His mind wandered back to that day almost three years ago, when Frank, his agent, left the hotel, and Thomas thought about what he could do. Frank had just shattered his dream of an exhibit. He then made a choice. Now Thomas wondered if he'd sold his birthright for a bowl of soup.

When he and James discussed their dad's will that gave the two of them equal share in anything left, James said they should let the hotel stand vacant until it could be sold, and they'd divide the profit. In the meantime, they'd share the worth of the house in Takoma Park. James wanted it, and if Thomas didn't, James would pay Thomas half of what it was worth, even though it would be in payments. Their dad had two cars, and they each should take one.

Thomas didn't want the house or another car. He had his black sports car, even though it was a few years old. James said that wasn't fair to Thomas. "It's your birthright, Thomas," James said. But Thomas was willing to give up his birthright for the hotel and his grandmother's Bible in which she kept the recipe for her famous soup with the secret ingredient.

Thomas said they had to make it legal, so they did. After they'd signed the papers Thomas wondered what in the world he'd done. He'd kept his studio. He had a small amount of money in his checking account but not enough to pay the heating bill for the hotel. He did have the two fireplaces and could afford wood for the rest of the winter. Without electric or gas he couldn't cook, but he could eat food that didn't need to be cooked. But for how long without money coming in?

Any royalties from reproductions wouldn't be available for months, if he earned any. He couldn't sell the hotel because that was his home and his studio, and he wouldn't want James to think he'd had that in mind all along so he'd get all the money from the sale.

He knew his grandmother would trade that recipe any day if it meant the welfare of her family. So he called around to hotels that had wanted to know about the soup that was advertised as the best anywhere. They weren't interested now because of their own financial difficulties. He called a major restaurant chain and was offered such a meager price he hung up on them.

With his education and experience he could get some kind of job. But he'd wanted the hotel for his painting. Why did God give him that talent if he couldn't use it? God? Well, sure. He'd believed in God all his life. He'd asked Jesus into his heart at an early age. So he'd do what Grandmother would say. He bowed his head and asked that God lead him. He knew he could exist, but did God have a plan? A reason to give him the ability and desire to paint?

So he went for a walk. Instead of fighting the Beltway traffic congestion he took the Metro subway into DC. He walked, looking at his surroundings, thinking about the paintings he'd done that were *good*. There was nothing wrong with that. The reproductions would bring pleasure to tourists, help them have fond memories of their visits to the area. Was that his purpose? If so, he'd try to accept it and be grateful. But he wasn't elated about it.

So he walked and thought, heedless of his whereabouts until he was no longer walking but was jerked off his feet when his head hit something hard, or something hard hit him. The next thing he knew he lay facedown on what felt to his face like sticky concrete but smelled worse. His blurry eyes finally made out the color red, and he realized that was his blood under his head. A hand was in his back pocket, and when its owner pulled out the wallet he swore and acted like he'd won the lottery, and his companion became a cheerleader.

Thomas pretended to be knocked out, which he felt like he was about to be, but sneaked a peek at them as they ran from the alley. He thought he'd seen them on the sidewalk earlier but gave them no thought except they looked like a couple teenagers looking for trouble by the way they swaggered and made remarks that he'd paid no mind to. At least he was alive, but his head throbbed, and he was going round and round into darkness.

The next thing he knew he opened his eyes and wondered if he was blind. Everything was dark. A voice said, "About time. Got you some coffee from the shelter. Better figure out if you can move. I don't share my place with just anybody."

Thomas didn't know if he was trying to joke or if that was a threat, but a vague shape began to come into focus and that seemed to be a grungy old man. Thomas sat up. "No broken bones, except my head feels like it's busted open. My watch," he said, feeling his bare wrist. "And my shoes."

"I got your shoes," the man said. "You can have them back. Just wanted to see how they'd feel." He chuckled. "Want to trade?"

A little moonlight filtered down, and Thomas was focusing better. The man held out the coffee. The cup felt warm. He took off the lid and drank half of it. He hadn't eaten since lunch, yesterday he supposed it was. Then he realized that may be the way this man thought many times. Seeing a pair of grungy sneakers, he picked one up. The sole flapped down about an inch and the fellow chuckled again.

Thomas decided to do the same and attempted to put it on his foot. In spite of his throbbing head, he laughed with the man as he forced his foot into it and his big toe stuck out about half an inch. They both seemed to think it better to laugh than cry. "You come here often?" Thomas said, tugging at the shoe. He got it off and set it aside.

"It's my home," the fellow said. "Like to be near the shelter where I go when the weather's too bad. It's a favorite for them punks, too. They leave somebody in here every once in a while."

"Alive?"

"Don't know nothing," the fellow said, and Thomas detected a stiffening of his attitude. He understood. What would a homeless man's word be worth anyway?

"I'm Thomas," he said, "And you're?"

The fellow shrugged and gave a little huff. He drank from his coffee cup.

"Think I'd better get my head checked."

The man took off the shoes, and Thomas thanked him.

"Shelter's around the corner. Here, they left this."

His wallet. He'd check it out when he had more light than a distant moon. This fellow could have kept it. "Thanks."

Thomas was warmly greeted at the shelter. A volunteer, who said he was Robert, cleaned the wound at the side of his forehead just below his hairline. "Not deep," Robert said, "just a lot of blood on your face and clothes." He seemed to know what he was doing; he pinched the cut together, placed a gauze pad over it, secured it, then wrapped gauze around Thomas's head like a sweatband.

Thomas washed himself off as best he could, brushed off the dirt, ate breakfast with the homeless, and watched the volunteers. He thought about his dad having liked the hotel he ran, a place where people paid for warm hospitality and to enjoy life. He'd wanted to turn Wildwood into a place much like that, but where those who couldn't afford to pay could go and also enjoy life. Just people, in a different place in life.

Right then, Thomas could identify with the homeless.

He couldn't identify with the volunteers.

He asked to borrow enough money to ride the Metro back

to Silver City, but Robert gave him the money and said it was not a loan but a gift.

He returned to the hotel, got cleaned up, and threw on jeans, along with a sweater that had been in a drawer for years simply because he didn't much care for it. He headed out, stopped at the bank for cash, went to a shoe store, bought a pair of sneakers too small for him, rode the metro, and waited in the alley until the man who helped him came home.

He held out the shoes.

The man's eyes widened. "Those for me?"

"Wanna trade?"

"These?" The man held up his foot, the sole of his shoe flopped, and he laughed.

"No," Thomas said. "Your story."

The man sat down with a heavy sigh. "Doesn't matter anymore."

"Does to me," Thomas said.

"Why?"

"I'm not sure," Thomas said.

The man huffed. "You want me to talk about what I try not to think about…for a pair of shoes?"

"You wouldn't believe what I've done for a bowl of soup."

They walked to the shelter for lunch. No questions were asked; the workers just filled his plate. The volunteers at the shelter wouldn't know him. Thomas had been educated at Georgetown. He'd spent a summer in Paris. He came from a well-to-do family. He'd run in different circles than those volunteers.

Volunteers only had love and kindness and hope and donated their time and money and caring to the needy.

Joe, the man's name, had been in prison most of his life because he hadn't had any better sense than to be with a buddy who was going into a store to pick up a six-pack. The clerk fought him, and his buddy pulled out a switchblade and didn't mean to, he said, but the clerk died. Joe was an accomplice.

Joe's family and friends had moved on with their lives, and Joe didn't fit in with society anymore.

Thomas told him there were places and people who could help, or homes where he could stay, and Joe said he didn't know anything about that, so Thomas helped him get into a halfway house.

Thomas thought about it that night in his bed in his studio in his empty hotel. Frank said he should paint what was in his heart. He knew how to love, how to care about other people, how to be helpful. But what was deep in his heart?

He wanted to paint.

He wanted his talent to be recognized as worthwhile. He didn't want Jesus to say someday, "You wicked and evil servant. You buried what I gave you."

Jesus gave one new commandment. Love one another. Love others as you love yourself. How could he paint from the heart if only ambition and himself were there?

Was he supposed to love the homeless? He could very well be one of them if he chose only to paint and not find a job somewhere. But that was no life to him.

Maybe he *should* paint and be one of them.

He laughed aloud at that.

Whoa!

That wasn't funny. That's actually an intriguing idea... .

He stopped himself again.

Don't even think like that, Thomas.

How could one love those people? Did Jesus love leprosy? Blind eyes? Crippled legs? No, but he loved the soul and eternal part of people that God created, the part that would never die. In other words, love wasn't loving or even liking the outside of a person. Love wasn't just feeling. Love was action.

At least, at least, he should try to find out who he was, what he was, whether he could care about others like those volunteers, whether or not he could be a more productive painter than thousands of other artists.

So he made a commitment to the Lord.

I'll be homeless and paint. I'll paint what is in the helpless and the homeless, and I'll paint what is in the caring, helping volunteers.

He would learn to love if it killed him.

In the three years out there, at times it almost did.

He went on a journey to find his heart.

At times he wondered if he cared because he was learning to paint from the heart. Or if he painted from the heart because he'd learned to care. He would let the Lord sort it out. Give that a pass or fail grade.

Since he'd returned, he'd begun reading his grandmother's Bible. It opened easily to the place where she'd kept her soup recipe on a folded piece of paper. More important to him now was her underlined passage, one he'd often heard her quote, "If I have not love, I am nothing."

He'd learned to love being homeless because it challenged his heart. That time on the street taught him how to be a giver and a receiver.

But for now, Thomas looked long at the paintings of Joe and Robert. The light was perfect today, so he set up the easel in the right spot and began to paint his latest subject. He liked to work in oils, but that would have been too difficult and expensive. He appreciated the effect he got from the watercolor. Instead of reflecting light, it bounced off the white paper and gave it a more luminous quality. That was the best medium for these paintings. It also eliminated the white pigment, so the painting looked cleaner than if he'd painted in oils, and it took less time to paint the portrait.

He smiled, thinking about his latest subject, Jim. His smile faded when he thought of Gloria. He mustn't allow thoughts of her to invade. She belonged...somewhere, but not in this particular project.

Chapter 20

All week Gloria and Thomas reviewed the résumés of the thirteen who wanted help and had set up appointments for the practice interviews. Thomas made them realize that the interviewers wanted and needed the unemployed as much as the unemployed needed a job. He emphasized they could ask what the representative had to offer them just as the rep could ask them that question.

Gloria remembered some of her own interviews. She'd given her résumé then waited like a beggar for a few pennies. She hadn't been ready.

Here, everyone was learning and being…personal. Heather volunteered to cut the hair of the residents instead of their being taken to a barbershop. The church decided to pay her. Caleb and Bobby were spending quality time together.

One morning after the practices, Thomas asked to watch her enter information on the computer since he'd been away from technology for a while. She did and remembered Clara saying, "Ask him."

Looking at the computer she said casually, "Thomas, are you working somewhere in the afternoons?"

"Every day but Sunday."

Just as she opened her mouth to ask what kind of job, he said, "But I don't get paid."

She looked over at him. "You…volunteer?"

He grinned. "You could call it that. I do it voluntarily. Now, what is this Twitter thing?"

She told him and demonstrated how shelters and the center could twitter each other, which reminded her. "Thomas, where do you sleep at night?"

"In a hotel."

Personal or not the question popped out. "How can you afford it if you have no job?"

"It's empty."

Oh my goodness. She immediately started telling him about Facebook and clicked in. Her thoughts ran rampant. If he broke into an empty hotel and slept there, and she knew it, she'd be legally and morally required to report him.

When she finally had nerve enough to gaze into his eyes again, she thought surely the mischief there and his broad smile wasn't satisfaction about breaking into an empty hotel.

She couldn't imagine that look was about…Facebook.

But she wasn't about to ask any more questions.

In the weeks that followed she looked forward to the mornings when they worked together, each teaching things to the other. Plans had to be finalized: how the church basement would be set up, which representatives would stay more than one day, who would stay with church members, who would need reservations at a motel, how long each session should last, which reps the interviewees would talk with so no one wasted valuable time.

Finally the day arrived. The job fair started on Thursday and would last through Saturday afternoon. Some representatives stayed the entire time. Some came for one day. Throughout the church basement long tables, covered with white cloths, were set up with two representatives at each table. Chairs were placed opposite them.

The first day was trial and error. For the most part, things went well. She and Thomas had tables set up near the door for the hundreds of unemployed to register and be given the names and table number of the representative most likely to be interested in their abilities.

The only ones that seemed suitable for Heather were a couple looking for clerks or waitresses. Caleb had been concerned about finding work all along, his only experience being tinkering with his car in high school and carrying a gun and throwing grenades in Iraq. He tried to joke about it, but his anxiety was obvious. Determined to do anything to help, Thomas suggested several possibilities, including James.

"James?"

"That's someone coming in tomorrow for a couple hours. Only the ones I picked will talk to him."

Gloria was afraid to ask if James might be involved with mechanics or guns.

On Friday afternoon a nice-looking man maybe in his midthirties, wearing a suit and tie, walked in. "Thomas," he said.

"James." Thomas looked at him rather askance and handed him a number.

James had the look of a man who'd been handed a rotten tomato.

"Your table is along the back wall."

Thomas must have wondered, as did she, whether or not James was going to go to the table. Thomas said, "I really appreciate this."

James nodded. "When I asked if you needed anything. I was thinking along a different line."

"Trust me," Thomas said.

"I'm trying."

Thomas nodded. "I know."

That sounded like a catch in his voice, and he looked away

from James, who grabbed Thomas's shoulder for a second and walked on back.

Gloria couldn't figure that one out. But for a brief moment, Thomas seemed as apprehensive as Caleb. The next instant he was again the competent, self-assured man who looked at the line and called, "Next, please."

Later, when James came by to leave, Thomas told her he was taking a break and the two walked out together.

Most unemployed came in the mornings, and the numbers dwindled as did the day. Late one afternoon Jim sat down with them.

"What do you think about our showing appreciation to the reps?" Thomas asked. "They could have just put ads in the papers."

Jim tightened his lips then lifted his brows. "I don't think you're saying *give them a hand.*"

Thomas smiled at Jim's chuckle. "I'm thinking dinner tomorrow night. A lot of the reps are staying over. We could invite them and those host families from the church."

"Takes money. Time. People."

"Not really. We can serve them in the dining room at the shelter. I'm sure several of the residents would like to serve. Cleanup would be on a volunteer basis. And as far as people"—he shook his head—"this menu can be cooked with only one…people." He pointed to himself.

Jim nodded and grinned. "Soup."

"Soup," Thomas repeated like it was the most precious word in the language.

Jim jumped out of his chair, excited. "I know Clara or Lois, or both, will be glad to make the rolls." He was already on his way as he said, "I'll print up the invitations and have them at their places in the morning."

Gloria could only stare.

"Don't worry," Thomas said. "You're invited to this fancy dinner." He winked. "Trust me."

She and James suddenly had something in common.

I'm trying.

The next evening Gloria took a final look at herself in the mirror and realized Thomas hadn't seen her wear anything but jeans and a T-shirt. On Sundays she attended the big church and he the Bible study at Wildwood. She wore a grass-green sundress with mock lace across the top of the bodice and at the hem. The basket weave necklace went well with the woven belt and wedge sandals. Her hair hung to her shoulders in a windblown, natural style, like that errant lock did all the time. She flicked it. Now it was welcome to fall freely.

Not that it mattered how Thomas had seen her dressed before. It was…just a thought.

After Jim let her and Clara off at the road in front of Wildwood, he drove to the church parking lot. Clara had removed the shoe boot but was being careful with her foot and dared not wear heels yet. As soon as they exited the car, Clara exclaimed, "Oh, that aroma."

Whatever it was smelled delicious. Clara stopped right inside the doorway, and Gloria stepped up beside her. "I couldn't imagine the dining room looking like this."

Clara nodded. "I've seen it before."

Gloria didn't know when it happened or where it all came from, but the tables were covered with white linen tablecloths with gold edging. Candles were lit in golden candleholders. Residents wore white aprons, as did Lois at the oven. Thomas in a white apron and chef's hat was stirring a caldron on the stove.

Where did all that come from? She feared she knew the answer. The hotel. He was a Robin Hood. But nowadays that was called a thief who could spend time in jail for his criminal activity.

"Come this way, please," a man said, grinning and eyes shining. That was Sam.

The same thing happened over and over as men in suits

and women in suits and nice dresses entered. After they were seated, Jim asked the blessing and the residents-turned-waiters put breadbaskets on the tables and served soup in bowls on plates she'd never seen before.

After the first bites the elegant diners became like oinkers in a pigsty. They exclaimed softly between bites, "Oh, what is this? I've never tasted anything like this. This isn't soup, it's heaven." They began to turn and look for the chef. Gloria handed her camera to Greg since the job fair was mainly an event sponsored by the church.

Greg zoomed and snapped while Thomas stood behind the countertop, smiling, and gave a little salute. After everyone paid their compliments to the chef, at the beginning instead of the end of the meal, she felt sure he looked at her with an expression of *you should have trusted me*.

Before long, he went around with a pot and ladle, offering refills. "Yes, please," she said as she moved the bowl to the side.

Very close to her ear he said, "You look lovely." He ladled her soup. "I won't say *tonight* because that would imply you haven't before."

She glanced around and up at him. Their gazes met and lingered for a moment. "Thank you," she said and slid her bowl over in front of her, wondering if anyone else at the table heard. But Jim, Clara, the preacher, and his wife were listening to Greg, on the other side of her, telling them about Turkey Trot. But so what if they heard? That was only the kind of casual comment anyone might make.

Gloria picked up her spoon and inhaled the wonderful aroma that quickened her pulses. Never would she have suspected she could become so enthralled by… by…soup.

Chapter 21 6

Monday morning, Gloria stayed busy with follow-up e-mails from some of the representatives who had further questions or needed information. A landscaper wanted to know how capable a couple of the residents were since she could use some men to do clearing and lifting. Some business wanted to make donations of goods or money. The job fair had been a tremendous success, and she began to believe Jim and Clara were right. She was needed. That was a good feeling.

Busy alone wasn't as much fun as with someone else. What she had resented when she and Thomas began working to-gether, she now missed. She still shuddered at the thought of dishes and tablecloths and aprons that could very well belong to a hotel. But she kept thinking he might at least pop in and mention the...soup.

Maybe his temporary status ended and he would move on to another volunteer project among the homeless.

She jumped when her phone rang. She started to reach for the desk phone and realized that it was her cell. She rarely got a call on it anymore. Her cell number was on her résumé form, which she managed to give to a couple representatives although she didn't sit for an interview. That probably explained the call.

She took the phone from her tote and stared at it while it rang. Raymond.

She thought about not answering. Surely he wouldn't call without a reason. Maybe the bookstore burned down and he suspected her. She'd been hot enough when she'd stalked out.

But that was then. This was now.

"Hi, Ray. What's up?" She did that just fine, but Jim walked in at that moment and, hearing her say "Ray," his brows formed their straight line.

Strange, she didn't have to deep breathe, steady a racing pulse, or have a stroke as she had imagined after he dumped her. The familiarity of his voice brought memories, mostly good. The last one had been the shocker.

"Chesapeake Bay area, huh?" she repeated for the benefit of Jim who sat in his chair looking relieved that she hadn't fallen apart.

"Well, I'm at work." Jim gestured toward the door, and she knew that meant she could leave if she wanted. "Are you really calling to find out where I work?"

He said not necessarily but would like to see her. "When? Okay. You remember where Aunt Clara and Uncle Jim live, I guess?"

He said of course.

Well, who knew? He hadn't remembered who his girlfriend was. Last Thanksgiving she'd visited at his parents' home. They all adored each other. At Christmas he visited with her at Clara and Jim's. He'd seemed a little uncomfortable at times, and she'd thought he might be nervous about giving her a ring. He didn't, so maybe Valentine's Day would be the time. After all, the gift of a ring usually follows talks about marriage and children and the best location to live considering their jobs.

Well, she got a shock when she went down to the storage

room to get a box of books and instead encountered Raymond and Stephanie bringing to life a kissing scene taken right out of a romance novel. Her gasp tore them apart, and Gloria tore out of there. They followed, with Raymond pleading for her to let him explain. She stopped, wondering if he'd make some lame explanation like Stephanie attacked him and he'd been surprised, but that wasn't what he said at all. He said, "We didn't mean for this to happen." Well, who forced them into the storage room?

Gloria stormed up the stairs. She would get no ring. She got the boot. And she kicked with it. Made a huge scene. Accused them of exactly what she'd suspected but had refused to believe.

It all became clear. After she told them off, with customers and workers listening and watching, she quit. Raymond pleaded. "This was one of the busiest seasons... ." Which set her off again. Yes, it *was* hearts and flowers season.

Everybody looked at her like she was the villain and had lost her senses. Didn't they know or care she'd lost the rest of her life she'd so carefully planned?

"You all right, honey?" Jim said after she told Raymond she'd meet him at the house.

She thought about that. "So far."

He'd be remembering her outbursts and crying jags. "I'll be praying for you," he said.

"Thank you." She left the office, thinking he'd prayed for her all her life. But Raymond still broke up with her. Was Raymond coming to ask forgiveness? Say Stephanie was a flirt, which Gloria knew, and he'd fallen for it? He'd had a weak moment? Why hadn't he had a weak moment with Gloria in the storage room?

She went inside the house and drank a cup of coffee with Clara and talked while waiting. Waiting for her emotions to boil over. What happened to those feelings? She and Clara talked mainly about the job fair since they'd already discussed her jilted situation for months up one side and down the other. Clara had always said, "Let God choose your mate." She really thought he had in the form of Raymond. She thought about changing clothes but decided she was *lovely* enough in her jeans and T-shirt and ponytail.

Raymond arrived in his nice car. Got out in his nice suit and nice tie. He looked nice, respectable, appealing, successful, like always. Clara came to the door, and they spoke politely. "I just wanted to talk with you, Gloria."

She went outside, and they walked along the sidewalk toward the church. She waited. "I want to apologize for the way things went down," he said.

"I accept," she said readily. "I don't want someone who doesn't want me." She glanced over at him. She wasn't angry about that. It was a fact. "It's the way it went down that hurt and angered and shocked me."

He glanced at her and nodded.

"Aunt Clara says I'll be stronger for it. I'm not sure why I must be stronger." She laughed lightly. "But Clara seems to think it an asset."

"Of course it is. And I'm not good enough for you."

"Oh, that's what all my friends said." She and her friends had called him inappropriate names and made up a few besides. She gave a little laugh again and he smiled, probably glad she wasn't ranting.

"But seriously, Raymond. It's not a matter of being good enough. Like the pastor said, we can't be good enough for God, just accept His love and blessings. Maybe when two people are meant for each other, that's what they do. Each one accepts and loves the other."

"We used to say we were meant for each other. You still think that?"

She was amazed at how calm and even...wise...she was feeling. Perhaps time and church and Clara and Jim had rubbed off on her.

"Yes." She watched his face turn troubled. That wasn't what he wanted to hear. He watched his shoes. "Raymond." He looked, and she smiled at him. "I think we were meant to meet, enjoy each other, and learn more about life and love. I don't regret our time together. And if Steph hadn't come along, maybe marriage for us would have been right. I don't know."

"Gloria, you're—"

She interrupted. "I know. You told me many times how wonderful I am."

He nodded and spread a hand as if helpless. She motioned, indicating they should walk through the church parking lot.

"I wanted to tell you that Steph and I plan to marry."

She waited for the anger or the tears. They didn't come. "I'm glad, Raymond." She really was. Glad it was serious between them and not just his floating from one girl to another or trying to further his own career. He was a nice guy.

"She's going to quit her job and stay home. I'll move into her position as regional manager. We'll need a district manager and a store manager. The assistant has handled the store since you left. Either job is yours if you want to come back."

The job, in which she'd felt secure, had enabled her to pay bills and generate a small savings. She could be promoted to district manager in this area. She could get a place close enough to be near Jim and Clara and get a substantial raise in pay. Since she'd be traveling a lot she could even live with them and pay rent.

"I won't be in the way," he said. "You might see me pop in a store occasionally and at meetings. But that's it."

She was doing fine seeing him now. "That wouldn't be a problem."

She motioned and they walked along a path near Wildwood leading to the creek. "And look, Gloria. I know I've said some crazy things. I joked about hooking up with Steph and that I knew she came from a wealthy family. It's not that. And she's not the snob we thought. That's a facade because of some tough times which left her with insecurities. But we want to make this work. Thanks to you, we may know how."

"Me?" She helped her boyfriend fall in love with another woman?

He looked at the treetops as they entered the wooded area. Then at the path. "You told me we couldn't have a successful life without God. I didn't mind acknowledging God but didn't take it too seriously. But Steph and I are going to start going to church and pursue this God thing."

"That's great, Ray. I'm really, really pleased for you."

They came out of the woods along the path next to the creek.

"Okay, any thoughts about the job? It will be a few months yet. Probably the first of the year."

She stopped, and he stood in front of her. After a silent moment he said, "Think about it, okay?"

"Yes. Thank you. I appreciate the offer."

"By the way, you said you were working."

"At that little church we just passed. It's a residence for homeless men."

His eyes held concern. "Is that safe?"

Safe? She looked at the creek, not as full and swirling as it had been in April, but still dangerous enough. "One of the residents got drunk over by that tree."

That tree. Somebody was sitting over there, leaning back against it, with a tablet propped at his knees. "He fell in, hit his head, and almost died. He has hallucinations."

"Aren't you afraid?"

When she first came to the center, she had been at least apprehensive. So much had changed. "Ray, I'm honored. That man served his country and his fellow Americans, me and you, in Iraq. He watched his buddy get blown to pieces." She hadn't analyzed it this way or felt the full impact until now. "He's in danger of losing his wife and son because of it. I'm afraid…I may not deserve the sacrifice he made."

Raymond looked contrite. "I'm sorry."

"I understand," she admitted. "When I rarely thought about them, I had all the stereotypical ideas about the homeless. And they weren't commendable."

He nodded. "I never imagined you doing something like that."

"Neither did I."

"Is it…my fault?"

"Yes." She looked him straight in the eyes. "And I'd like to thank you."

He shifted uncomfortably from one polished black shoe to the other. Gloria reached out and touched the sleeve of his suit coat. "No, really. I mean it. This is good for me. Thank you for the years we had together. And for being honest with me now."

"I did—"

She put out her hand to stop his words. "You can find your way back, can't you?"

He said he could and she said, "You'll make a wonderful husband for…Steph."

"Thank you." He took her hand in his and held it while taking slow steps away, and then let it go.

She watched what she once considered her future walk away and disappear into the woods. The entire time they talked she had not felt…devastated, or…enthralled. Turning, she looked at a figure leaning against a tree and walked toward it. He looked up at her and said, "Hello."

She smiled. "That was my former security," she said. "He offered me my job back or a promotion with a raise in pay."

Chapter 22

Thomas figured the safest question to ask was, "He's your former boss?"

"That, too." She gave a small laugh. "I haven't thought of him as my boss since changing my major from English to business management so he'd hire me to manage the bookstore. But for at least two years he was my…" She studied the sky as if it might give her the word. "Steady. Yes, we went steady. Until…"

She began with the storeroom, her conniption fit, walking out, the inability to find another job, spending her savings, being forced to live with Clara and Jim, the despair, and having pity parties for weeks.

"Losing those you love is no picnic," he said, watching her walk toward the drop-off.

Her face turned toward him. "I loved who and what he was. Like Greg in a way, only more mature. A great guy, fun, intelligent, successful, nice-looking, decent."

Was she now falling for Greg? He hadn't thought so. But she had seemed more accepting of her work and him in the past weeks. "Sounds ideal," he said.

She nodded. "Right. Like heroes in some of the romance novels in the bookstore."

He wondered if she meant her steady was ideal or had been fantasy.

Her gaze fastened on the tree under which he sat. "He traveled a lot so we always looked forward to being together again. We confirmed how right we were for each other, talked about the best location for a house considering our jobs, what kind of home we wanted, having children, saving enough money to get a good start, stuff like that."

"Sounds serious."

She nodded. "It was, at the time. That's why Raymond felt he needed to come and say his official good-bye."

"Sure you're all right?"

Her glance met his, and he shifted his gaze from her standing there on the high part of the bank down to the fast-flowing creek and back at her.

She laughed lightly and stepped back. "Oh no. I no longer think my life is over. Just a time for a new beginning." Her gaze moved to the little white clouds drifting away from them across the blue sky as if her past was doing that. She spoke softly and reflectively. "When I began to get over the shock and anger, I realized my grief was over my loss of security and what Raymond represented instead of Raymond himself."

She stepped away from the bank. "I can remember the story. But I've…closed the book."

He knew that feeling, too. "Are you thinking of taking the job offer?"

"It's not available until first of the year. I need to support myself, so I'll think about it. Oh, in the meantime, I need to keep this job. I'd better see if I can scrounge up a sandwich and get back to work."

Thomas stood and brushed off the back of his jeans. "I could use a sandwich myself. Mind if I join you?"

"I'll even make the sandwich for you. After the way I told my life story. I didn't really mean to—"

"Don't apologize, Gloria. I'm glad you did. No one heard you but me and the birds and the squirrels and the snakes."

She grimaced at that then smiled.

"You can trust me."

She laughed then, and her eyes were touched by the same sunlight that put that reddish-gold sheen on her hair. "Anyone who can be trusted to turn soup into a successful dinner may be trustworthy in other things."

They walked along the path that Raymond had taken. She must have thought about him since she became reflective again. She sighed. "I didn't know that one could really fall in love without meaning to, that it happened without one's intending it."

His glance was quick. Was she falling for…Greg, after all? Just as quickly she spread her hands and color came into her cheeks. "That's what happened with Raymond and Stephanie. Just, *ping,* out of the clear blue sky." And *ping,* she asked, "You ever been in love?"

"Depends on what definition one has of it, I suppose." She'd been so open about Raymond, he should respond with a little honesty of his own. "That occurred to me after I began dating a gorgeous brunette in college. But later, my wanderings became a priority. And love can be confused with something else."

Her eyes questioned. "I mean, like kisses," he said. "They can be a physical thing, not necessarily a love thing."

She didn't dispute that, and he refused to look at her lips as if he didn't have a photographic memory or an imagination.

They reached the church, went into the kitchen, raided the refrigerator, and made their sandwiches. "We can sit at a table," she said. "Jim had said I could take today off if I wanted, but I'm anxious to see what comes in about the job fair."

"We did all right with that." He sat in a chair adjacent to her. "We should celebrate."

Gloria had shared some of her innermost thoughts. Maybe he should reveal a few things about himself. It might not go over well if one of these days he acted like Clark Kent who would fling off his eyeglasses, rip his shirt open, and shout, "Guess who and what?" He doubted anyone would see a Superman emblem on his T-shirt.

"Let's go out to dinner somewhere. Really, Gloria," he said sincerely. "You helped me more than you know. I'd like to do something for you."

She didn't balk, but she did take a while chewing her sandwich. She swallowed and sipped her tea. "Thomas, you've helped me equally, if not more than I helped you. But I don't know if this would be allowed."

"Allowed?"

"I'll ask Jim."

Then he understood. She'd confided in him as if he were a friend or a confidant. Or maybe she'd been talking to the tree where he happened to be sitting. She was an employee, and he a homeless man. He'd forgotten that for a while. She hadn't. He thought a moment. "I'm not a resident. Not staying here overnight. Seems I'm more a volunteer, don't you think?"

She was thinking. After a moment she shrugged. "Well, if we do this, it has to be dutch treat."

She said *if.* He jested. "Can you afford it on that minimum wage you complain about?"

"I could afford bread. But since you don't have a job, you can bring the water."

"Sounds like a plan."

"But," she said, "a lot does depend on where we'd go."

"Tell you what. I'll pick the place and you pick the time. I would like it to be a cool evening."

"Weather?"

"That, too," he said, and they grinned and bit into the sandwiches. He liked to see the happiness in her eyes, even if she wasn't canvas material that way.

Watching her pick away some of her sandwich bread, he liked the closeness of their having formed a bond while working together over the past weeks. Maybe they could progress to the level of being friends.

But she had not sought him out. He'd happened to be at the base of the tree at a time when she needed to talk and confide as she closed her book on Raymond. That had been a vulnerable moment for her.

Oh really?

If she was the vulnerable one, why had it been he who extended a dinner invitation?

192
124
——
68

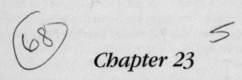

Chapter 23

Jim entrusted more of the office work to Gloria, talked about retiring and limiting himself to resident counseling and teaching Bible studies at the center and church. The daytime RA expressed interest in the directorship. Jim and he were spending a lot of time together. Clara had cut back considerably on her volunteering but still sent her pies and special treats.

Gloria started going in a little earlier and sometimes had breakfast with Thomas after the men ate. She shared correspondence she received about jobs having been filled as a result of the fair. The landscaper hired two of the residents part-time. After school started for Bobby, Heather could begin working mornings at a hair salon in a Walmart only about fifteen miles away. Helping Clara at Bible school during the summer had given her more confidence.

Gloria knew job fairs were always successful for many, but she'd been part of this one and felt great about it. She got a slight raise in pay but still not enough to be on her own.

Some mornings she'd simply go in and say hi to everyone. "Hot this morning," someone might say. She'd reply, "Dog days of summer." Sometimes she'd fan her face with her hand.

She and Thomas would grin at each other. Neither mentioned the dinner again, but the days were getting cooler.

"You're unusually quiet tonight," Jim said one night at supper.

"Thomas asked me to have dinner with him," she said as if he'd asked today instead of weeks ago. "What do you think?"

He didn't look surprised. "I think you should say yes or no."

She glanced at the ceiling and back at him and said, "That's a huge help." Clara shook her head as if he was hopeless.

"But if you want to know what I think of him," Jim said, in a serious tone. "I like and respect him." He nodded. "Very much."

Clara added, "I've only seen and heard good things about him. I think he's a fine young man."

Gloria felt her face grow warm. Why the glowing recommendations? "It's only...dinner."

Jim shrugged. "Right. Some dinners are just dinners. Then there's...soup."

"Oh!" Gloria said, and they all began to laugh. "Please, let's change the subject. Clara, those marigolds and asters are looking great, aren't they?"

So one colorful, cool day during the third week in October she walked up to the countertop, looked at Thomas, hugged her arms, and said, "Brrrr."

Maybe he forgot. Or it didn't matter now. After a moment of studying her while she grew warmer, he said, "I thought I might freeze to death before it was cool enough for you. However, the reservations were made weeks ago and the table is waiting."

His playfulness had a way of easing tension. "Tomorrow night? Seven?"

"I'll pick you up at Jim and Clara's."

In what? Jim's truck? But that was not for her to question. Even if he walked from the center to Jim's, and they walked back to the center and ate there, it would be fine. This was his way of saying thank you. This was…ridiculous. But it couldn't lead anywhere. Surely he didn't think that. And like Jim had said, there were always the words *yes* or *no.*

She chose to wear brown pants, a matching cami, and a quarter-length sleeved, yellow knit, low-cut fitted sweater with a brown belt, layers of gold chains, and a pendant necklace, and dangling gold loop earrings. She was pleased with the sporty but dressy look that would be suitable for about any place they might go. She'd bought the outfit last fall to wear after Raymond returned from a trip. She'd worn it once to church.

After approving her shoulder-length hair and applying a bright lipstick, she slipped into her wedged sandals. Getting dressed for an evening out felt good. She just hoped she hadn't overdone it.

She thought not when Jim opened the door to Thomas. Amazing how nice a bearded man with a ponytail could look. No, nice was how Raymond looked, and he had given her a few lessons in men's clothing. Thomas looked…cool in khaki Chinos and a light and dark brown argyle sweater over a light-colored shirt, maybe ecru or beige, unbuttoned at the neck. She thought they looked pretty good for a minimum-waged woman and an unemployed man.

She felt like she'd opened up a suspense novel in which the unexpected occurred, and she wondered what might happen next.

That book became a mystery or maybe a true detective novel when she saw the car. A sports car?

"Where'd you get this?" she managed to say, after they were inside and he started the engine.

"From the garage at the hotel."

She gasped. He grinned.

He drove down the street and turned at the end, heading toward the main road. "Do you remember the man who came to the job fair for a couple hours on Saturday but wasn't listed and that I sent a few job-seekers to him?"

The one he hadn't addressed formally and had walked outside with.

"James?"

"He's my brother."

So his brother was nearby? This was his brother's car? Maybe he was staying with his brother. But he'd said he was staying at a hotel. Mystery.

In no time at all they were right outside Silver City, and he turned into the driveway of what looked like a bed-and-breakfast, or a…small hotel. No lights shone from the windows. He drove around to the back where lights glowed from several windows. The car clock registered two minutes before seven.

"Thomas?" She exited the car and walked up to him. "Is this the empty hotel you mentioned?"

"It is." He led her to the back door, moved aside the Closed sign, unlocked it, opened it, and gestured for her to enter.

"You sure this is all right?" she whispered as if the police or someone might hear.

"Gloria, did you notice I unlocked the back door with a key?"

Did he notice that didn't do much for her uneasiness? At the same time, this was rather intriguing. They walked slowly along the cool hallway, past closed doors. He stopped at a door and faced her. "This hotel has been closed for over three years. But it has been in my family for decades. The last owner was my dad."

Had been? Was? It was all too confusing, but his moment of sadness seemed to change abruptly, and he smiled. "Let's enjoy our dinner, shall we?"

He opened the door, and she gasped as she walked in. This was a cozy living room. A round table, covered by a white cloth with gold fringe and highlighted by flickering candles in golden holders, sat between two couches and across from a fireplace. The fire danced and licked the wood with delightful sounds and emitted an odor of warmth and wood and coziness on a…cool evening.

This was more than cool. It was wonderful. Better than any restaurant.

Her glance swept around the room, taking it all in. There were three seating arrangements of a couch and two chairs, end tables with lamps, coffee tables, a piano in a corner, and beautiful paintings on the walls.

Thomas pulled out a chair from the table. She sat. He walked over and sat opposite her. Okay, who needed food in a setting like this? But a middle-aged man in black pants, white shirt, and a towel over his arm came in and set two glasses of water at their places.

Thomas introduced him as Blackston, a waiter when his dad ran the hotel. Blackston asked how she liked her steak and silently left to fulfill her request. Thomas began to tell her the story of his dad's success, then his losing so much, including his life.

"James and I divided up what was left. Although James thought I got the worst end of the deal, I wanted the hotel and grandmother's soup recipe with the secret ingredient that became the hotel's trademark."

When Blackston appeared again, Thomas said, "Hope you don't mind I ordered for you."

Looking at the meal set before her, she thought she could live with it. "We'll see," she teased, loving the smell and looks of it. Blackston set out the appropriate drinks to accompany the meal Thomas described. A light frisée salad with bacon shallot vinaigrette and a filet mignon with garlic frites. After Thomas said a blessing, she began to eat and thought her moan of pleasure reassured him about having ordered for her. It was a perfect meal without featuring large portions that made one feel overstuffed.

"This may not be the kind of dinner conversation you want."

"I've wanted to know about you, Thomas, but wasn't sure I should ask."

She listened, fascinated as he told his hopes, his dreams, his failings and successes in every area of his life, his commitment to the Lord, and his having no idea how it all might end.

He finished his story. So he was one of those starving artist types. She'd often heard that creative people were odd, or at the least…eccentric. But having worked in a bookstore, she knew that some wrote very good books.

Thomas obviously could work at many jobs and make a good living. But it was also clear he'd rather paint, even if it meant he might starve.

Blackston came in with cappuccino soufflés. Thomas finished his before she did. She wanted to savor the flavor as long as possible.

"There's something I want to ask you," he said. "Excuse me, I'll be right back."

What did he have in mind? Ask if they could see each other in a personal way? Like tonight. She loved this. Her heart beat fast.

This was a magical night.

Chapter 24

Thomas returned with a large notebook. "You said you majored in English before changing to business management?"

She nodded.

"I've written a few things about the homeless. I wondered if you might read what I wrote and give your opinion. If you have time or...want to?"

Gloria took the notebook and settled in a chair facing the fireplace to see the writing better. It was handwritten. Thomas switched on the end table lamp.

He sat on the nearby couch. She read one, two, three, entries then turned to the first one again. These were short biographies of homeless people: name, age, how the person became homeless. What the person was doing to get out of that situation.

She flipped through a few others. They were all about the same format, although the stories were different.

Most had notes stapled to them, telling where the homeless person is now and what they're doing. Some did not.

She read one about a night volunteer. He had been homeless, later returned to school in middle age, became a grade-school teacher, retired, and now wanted to identify with and help the homeless.

She closed the notebook and sat for a moment with her hands folded on the binder, uncertain what to say. Glancing up, she saw the inquisitive look on his face, his questioning eyes. Waiting.

"These are touching stories. I've heard many like this since I've been here."

"But?" He leaned forward, his forearms on his knees.

"But…" she continued, "when I hear their stories, I see them. I see their expressions, their mannerisms, how they're dressed. I see their poverty. I see embarrassment or hope or hopelessness."

He nodded, understanding. She went on. "Each of these could be turned into an article for a magazine and maybe inspire others to donate time or money. Number two for instance. You say the woman is twenty-three. Her handwritten note says she is now working in a department store and gets her clothes at a discount. She said you wouldn't know her now. She even got a perm."

He grinned like she was telling him something great instead of criticizing. She pressed further. "I'd like to know how she looked when she was homeless. In my mind, I can see her on the floor of a department store in nice clothes and her hair curly. But I don't see her homeless."

"Great analysis," he said. "Maybe I'm doing what I intend. I don't want those words"—he pointed at the notebook—"to give the reader a picture of how she looked when she was homeless. I want to know if my factual account could be worded better. You see"—he took a deep breath—"that life— that embarrassment, hope, or hopelessness, and the caring of the volunteers—should be in the paintings. Otherwise…"

She saw the uncertainty in his eyes when he began again.

"Otherwise, I will have to answer what the past three years were all about."

She looked down wondering, would it be embarrassment and hopelessness for him? "May I see them?"

"Not yet. I don't want opinions one way or another until the project is finished. It's almost there. Everything I have inside me, in talent and work, is in those paintings. And I don't know if they will be good enough. Homeless people aren't good enough for most people in this world. So can I expect paintings of them to be?"

Homeless people aren't good enough. She felt quite warm, and it wasn't because of the dying fire in the fireplace.

She was afraid…he was right.

"So…what will you do if they're not good enough?"

He shook his head. "I can't dwell on that yet. Just…continue until it's done."

There was no reason to linger. Talk about what kind of music or books or movies or activities they liked would seem trivial after an evening of someone sharing his innermost yearnings. The car clock read 9:32 when he returned her to Clara and Jim's.

She touched his hand on the wheel before he could reach to switch off the engine. "Don't get out," she said. He turned his hand, and she gave it a little squeeze. "Thank you."

His expression was warm. "My pleasure."

They said good night. She had touched him physically, without worrying about what he might think, what she might think. She got out with the notebook and upon opening the front door heard the car drive away.

Clara and Jim sat in the living room, each with their reading material. She sat on the couch near Clara. Jim broke the silence. "Is this a little early to be home from a date?"

She shook her head. "I think I may be a little late." She wasn't referring to the evening. How to say it? "Tonight was the most romantic evening I've ever spent with anyone." She told them about the room, the fire, the candlelight, the food, the waiter, having an entire hotel to themselves.

"And yet," she said, still feeling the wonder of it, "it wasn't about romance at all. I began the evening wondering who and what is Thomas. And what is this to me, if anything? But it ended with getting me out of the way, really seeing someone else's dreams and hopes and purpose. I saw the heart of a homeless person." She scoffed lightly. "Even if it is self-imposed homelessness."

They were just listening, like they'd done when she ranted and raved about Raymond and her job. Then they had given advice and wisdom. Right now they were just…looking.

"I do care about other people and the residents."

"We know that," Clara said.

"Uncle Jim, you told me they were just people. But I still saw them first as labels more than people. I'm probably not making any sense."

They didn't say anything, but their expressions, like always, shone full of love and acceptance. "I may be several months late on this, but thank you for offering your home and your love." She stood. "I accept."

Still holding the notebook she went over to each, kissed their cheeks, and told them she loved them. Looking back over her shoulder at the doorway, she saw them gazing at her. Did they think she'd lost her mind?

Or…found her heart?

$$\frac{192}{134}{58}$$

Chapter 25 6

The weather turned cold and windy and rainy the last of October. November winds and rain and fog seemed to beat and hover about Thomas's studio windows. He hadn't turned on the gas yet, and the small electric heater left a lot to be desired. But the small royalties Frank sent him had to be dispersed carefully. On foggy days natural light no longer came through the windows, so he had to use electricity.

There was plenty of firewood in the dry space under the hotel, but he'd finished all the sketching and did his painting in the studio. Sometimes he wondered if what he heard was his bones shaking instead of the wind rattling the windows. Frank and his wife were coming to spend a week with James and Arlene and the children. Thomas wouldn't have to pack up his paintings and haul them into DC but would get the agent's approval or disapproval right there in the studio.

Thomas knew he hadn't sounded confident when he called and told Frank he'd be ready for him to see his work of three years. Frank hadn't sounded too excited either. He just said, "We'll see, Thomas. I hope we can work something out."

That was polite. No nepotism involved. Maybe being the

man's son-in-law's brother got his foot in the door, but it didn't get his paintings sold.

He didn't know how he could have gotten along without Gloria to work on the written part of the project. He'd never been that great with typing, but she was a whiz on the computer, and Jim told her to use any free time on the project. She often worked after hours. He appreciated her more every minute but didn't have time to think about it.

He'd pop in after breakfast and say, "Now which one is number five and which is number six? He was in the framing stage and wanted to keep them in order. After the second day, when he stuck his head in the door, she held out a sheet of paper with the paintings listed in the order he had them in the notebook.

"How can I ever repay you?" he said.

"You can't. I'm a volunteer." She squinted and shot him a mean look. "But I want you to know I gave up the Turkey Trot for this."

"Gloria, no. I don't want you giving up anything."

"You don't want me to give up gobbling all day and running like a turkey, mainly away from Greg?"

Maybe he did, aware of how appealing she looked with that color appearing in her cheeks, but before he thought of how to answer she said, "Seriously though, the church has plenty of runners. They'll raise a lot of money without me. And there will be plenty of girls to run with Greg. He's quit pursuing me anyway."

"Well, thanks for the list. I have framing to do."

He finished the day before Thanksgiving except for setting up the display and including the notebook. On Thanksgiving he helped the church, along with Jim, Clara, Gloria, and many volunteers, serve Thanksgiving dinner to the center residents, area homeless, and anyone wanting or needing a meal. They served from noon until after dinnertime.

All the eaters were happily stuffed and the volunteers

happily filled and exhausted. Gloria took many pictures that would continue to keep awareness of the needy before the public.

When the clean-up crew took over, Thomas walked out with Gloria, Jim, and Clara who said it was time to get a Christmas tree now that Thanksgiving was over.

"We need one for the center," Jim said. "You want to take my truck and get two about yea big?" He lifted his hand above his head.

Thomas nodded. "I could use a yea big one in the hotel living room and one about four feet taller in the dining room. Go with me, Gloria? You don't work tomorrow, do you?"

"No, but I'm watching Bobby tomorrow morning. Heather and Caleb have an appointment with a psychologist. They're hoping to be back together by Christmas."

"Caleb's doing well at the center," Jim said. "Taking classes, helping out. No nightmares."

"Heather's mother is being supportive now," Clara said. "She's realizing Caleb's problem isn't alcohol but the traumatic experiences."

Thomas had an idea. "Bobby would probably like going. Bring him along."

Gloria glanced at Jim. "That little seat behind the driver safe for him?"

"Oh yes," Jim said.

"You don't want to pick out your tree, Clara?" Gloria asked.

"No. Jim does that. I do the decorating."

"But I don't do it if somebody else does it for me," Jim said.

"Sounds like fun," Gloria said. "My roommate and I always had a little rinky-dink artificial one. But," she added, "Heather talked about their getting one. They might want to do it as a family."

Thomas nodded. "Bobby could pick out some he likes and tell them about them."

That settled it, and early the next morning they bundled

in their jeans, jackets, scarves, and hooded jackets in case it turned colder or wet. By mid-morning it was mildly cold with a sky that threatened rain or snow.

Thomas took them to a lot right outside Silver City where his family always got their trees. They'd gone down a couple rows and Bobby was favoring the huge ones.

They stepped to the side when a woman approached pushing a baby buggy. She started to pass; then her eyes got big and she stopped to cry out, "Thom…aaaas?"

"Libby?" He stared a moment, then glanced at Gloria and back again at the attractive brunette.

"Is that you under there?" she asked, her gaze sweeping over his beard.

"Almost. Right now I'm incognito. This is Gloria. Bobby. Libby." He looked down at the baby carriage where an infant was bundled up tightly and sound asleep. "That's…yours?"

"Afraid so. And to my surprise, I love being a mom." The baby stirred and opened its eyes and fussed. She moved the carriage back and forth, and the baby closed its eyes again. "Meet Teddy Morton II."

"Ted?" He'd worked as bellboy at the hotel and had led Thomas into a rather wild life. Thomas caught himself before he said, "You mean the overweight teddy bear who was a cutup and barely got out of high school and never went to college but went to work at some air-conditioning plant?"

His eyes must have asked it. She nodded. About that time, a lean, good-looking fellow walked up, stuck out his hand, and gushed, "Well, if it ain't the long-lost, most-likely-to-succeed hometown boy come back. Heard you was around somewhere. How you doing, buddy?"

"Not as well as you, apparently."

"Well, we'll just have to get together and talk about it. I can always use another good hand." He punched Thomas in the bicep. "Kidding, bro. Well, not really. Would you believe I'm a millionaire now?"

"You mean…having Libby and Junior here?"

He fluffed that off with a wave of his hand. "Ah, that goes without saying." He gave Libby a grin, and she grinned back like it was true. "Is that one yours?" He looked at Bobby. "If he is, you work fast and grow 'em big."

Thomas introduced Gloria and Bobby as friends of his.

Ted turned to Gloria and spoke to her as if she were the only one there. "After Thomas dumped Libby, I called her, found her, and told her I wanted to help her get over her broken heart." He turned back to Thomas. "Wanted to do you a favor, bud. Anyway, started my own heating and air-conditioning business. Done a lot of crawling around in soot and ashes. But you know how people are, always too hot or too cold. I now have businesses in four counties and moving on."

One could never be sure when Ted was telling the truth. Thomas looked at Libby. She nodded and held out her left hand. On her ring finger sat an enormous diamond. Glancing back at her he saw her eyebrows wiggle. She was a happy woman.

The baby fussed again. Ted reached over, nudged Libby's hand away, and began rolling the carriage back and forth. "Well," he said, "we better get Teddy Bear home before his little nose freezes to death. By the way, thanks for giving up the most beautiful, wonderful girl in the world."

Thomas didn't think he should say it was his pleasure.

Ted glanced at Gloria. "But I see you got another one. Don't let her get away. By the way, I go to the same church as James. He's a big dude there."

"Aren't you?"

He grinned. "I fix a lot of furnaces and air conditioners. Just a common laborer."

Thomas laughed and shook his head. "And taking their money."

"I work for it. At least, my crew does. Want a job?"

"Afraid I'd be lost in that kind of work."

Ted nodded. "That's okay. You white-collar people just keep lining my pockets. But I'm in the phone book. We'll get together. You ever need anything, let me know."

Thomas knew he meant that. He had a thought. "I know somebody who might make you a good worker. Bobby's dad."

"Send him over."

Thomas knew if there was any way, Caleb now had a job. They said their good-byes.

"She's...the one," Gloria said, instead of asking, keeping her eyes on Bobby across the aisle examining the cones on a pine tree.

"Yep. When Libby and I decided to part ways, she was planning to get her master's degree and teach college courses. She may someday, but she seems pretty content being a wife and mom."

"I guess that happens when you fall in love and marry."

"Surprising in a way. They're from two different worlds. But they sure seem to complement each other. But"—he shrugged—"he wasn't one of my crowd when we met. He worked for us as a bellboy. I liked being around him, and we became friends. I'd like to renew that friendship." He thought a minute. "But that would involve Libby. Think that would be okay?"

She shrugged. "A lot may depend on"—she cast him a side-long look—"on what kind of kisses you two shared."

"Physical or love, huh? Well, it's pretty obvious I pursued the paintbrush instead of Libby."

She nodded and walked over to Bobby.

What might Gloria be thinking? He obviously still pursued the paintbrush over anything and anybody else.

Seeing that little family and watching Gloria with Bobby made him think about having that kind of life for himself one of these days.

He walked over to Gloria and Bobby. "Yes, when I broke up with Libby, my commitment was to my painting. But three years ago my commitment became to let that paintbrush be used by God for His glory, His purpose. That's not the kind of commitment one backs away from. Not and have any kind of life at all."

He had no idea what that conveyed to her, or if he'd meant for it to. But after a glance at him she said, "Ooops, there he goes."

They took off after Bobby who was jumping up and down. "This one's gotta be it. Mom and Dad will love it."

"We'll have the attendant put it aside for your parents to look at," Thomas said. "But I agree. I think this one...is just right. What do you think, Gloria?"

She gave him a quick glance. "I agree. Now we'd better find the right ones for the hotel."

"I've already seen one that looks perfect for the living room."

"Then we'd better grab it before somebody else does."

Yes, that could happen. With trees and...with people.

192
141
—––
51

Chapter 26

Early Saturday morning, Gloria drove through the cold rain to the hotel. Thomas said he had boxes of ornaments his family always used but had no idea how to decorate the trees. He'd thought decorations magically appeared on the trees, but the ornaments were family keepsakes.

Her rinky-dink artificial tree had come with tiny, clear lights. She had, in the past, helped hang ornaments on trees a few times. On Friday evening she watched Jim and Clara decorate.

She parked at the back of the hotel, hurried inside, and hung her jacket on one of the back door hooks. She found the dining room and was surprised at how big it looked. Maybe that's because no patrons sat around at tables, the chandeliers remained off, and the open drapes presented only a rather dim gloom.

They'd be decorating a tree in a cold room in an empty hotel. That thought saddened her. But after he got the lights on, moved the ladder, and began to read the notes that accompanied many of the ornaments, she realized the dining room wouldn't be empty. It would be as full of memories as Thomas was as he talked about his family. His mom, dad, and grandmother. All gone from this world but alive in his heart and mind.

He really didn't need her help from the moment he said, "Maybe we should put the ribbon on before we attach the ornaments." He asked her opinion at each turn or twist, but she saw his creative flair from the very first. Even before they started with the ornaments, the tree was looking as good as any fancy tree in a department store window.

When they finished and turned the lights on, it was like the gray light and rain outside the windows hurried away in deference to the beauty that could light up a room like nothing else.

They kept looking at it and each other, grinning and nodding.

Finally he turned his head to glance around the room. "I wanted to brighten this room since I'll be hanging my paintings on the walls and setting some around for my agent to view. Think this will do it?"

She tried to push away the thought, *The tree should be quite a contrast to paintings of homeless people.*

That fleck of rare insecurity touched his eyes for a moment. She quickly turned and walked over to the wall, looking at the paintings already hanging there. Some were landscapes around the Washington area, others depicted memorials, the White House, public buildings, the hotel, a cherry tree that could be one on the front lawn, and some places she didn't recognize. Then she realized the creative scrawl in the corner of the paintings were all the same, and there seemed to be a definite *K.* "Did you paint these?"

He didn't sound thrilled at admitting that he had. She turned toward him. "I think they're...wonderful."

He nodded and stepped over to a display rack near a corner and gave it a little spin. "That's what Frank says. Good enough to be reproduced and sold to tourists. Like hundreds, thousands of other artists." He shrugged. "But..." He smiled. "Thank you."

She stared at the lighted tree, hardly aware that Thomas was stacking boxes and taking them to a closet in the alcove beyond the fireplace. That little word, *but,* held a world of meaning. He didn't want to be like thousands of others. He wanted the Lord to use his gift in a special way, to make a difference. All this gave her a different view of her parents. They made a commitment to follow the Lord's leading to the mission field. She'd resented it at times. But now that seemed like such an immature, selfish way of viewing it. She couldn't have had a better life with them than she had with Clara and Jim. She'd lacked nothing.

"What's on your mind?" Thomas said, going over to un-plug the lights.

"My parents."

"Shall we decorate the tree in the living room?"

She was glad to leave the dining room that had looked gloomy again with the tree lights off. The living room was entirely different. One could settle down in there, alone, and still love it. The fireplace was blazing, the room warm and cozy. He made hot cocoa, and their mood began to catch the spirit of the upcoming season as they talked and laughed about childhood memories of Christmases past.

When he walked with her to the back door, his thoughts turned again to the meeting with Frank. She shrugged into the jacket he held as he said, "Will you sit in on the meeting with Frank?"

She felt sure her shock showed. He said quickly, "Frank will need to see how the book complements the paintings. You've done all the work there."

"But it's your work. All I've done is type and print."

"You took a mess of words and made sense of them. But I've imposed on you enough."

"We're friends, Thomas." Their gazes held for a moment before she looked down and decided to fasten her jacket just to keep from looking into his eyes like that. He needed her to be there? To be supportive? She thought she might be more afraid of what Frank might say than Thomas was. But he was right. She had typed the pages. "Sure. If you think it's okay, I'll be there. And even if Frank doesn't like them, it's not the end."

"No. But these past three years represent my best, my heart, my commitment to the Lord. If Frank thinks they won't go, they won't. I can still paint. I'll accept my talent is limited and adjust. I'll serve the Lord in whatever way He allows. His plan is best, even if I don't understand it or like it."

She nodded. "Like me losing Raymond and my job and my security. I hated that. And although I didn't really ask God about it, I just assumed it was right. I see that my plan may not have been best. Maybe Raymond and I could have made it. But, anymore, I don't want to settle for just…making it."

"That's how I feel about my painting. Like the biblical character said—Job, I think—I'll serve him, 'though he slay me.' " He laughed at that. "I think it would be easier if he'd just slay me."

"If Frank says no, you'll be okay?"

"Not really. But I will serve the Lord in whatever way He allows. His plan is best even if I don't like it. All I have to do is look around and know how blessed I am. I learned three years ago how easy it is to feel that you have no one and nothing."

She needed to get out of there before she cried. This was hard, seeing someone's life's work, someone's heart's desire, and not knowing what would happen with it. She would go to the office and finish the book today. "The pages will be ready for you Monday morning."

She thought he might ask if she liked it. But that wouldn't make any difference. Frank's opinion would be the deciding factor. "It does need one more entry." At his questioning eyes she said, "You."

"Oh no. It's not about me. It's about the homeless and the volunteers."

"It's all about you, Thomas." She opened the door and left him staring at her.

He closed the door after she settled into the car, and she sat there a moment. In a few days this would end. She and Thomas had talked about what might happen if Frank rejected his work.

Neither had mentioned what would happen if Frank accepted it.

If he did, Thomas would fly off to Paris or wherever famous artists went, and she'd maybe take Raymond's job offer.

If Frank didn't accept the project, then Thomas would live in an empty hotel and volunteer at the center, and she would have to take Raymond's job offer.

But she needed to get this project over with, one way or another, and keep her mind off someone whose commitment was to a paintbrush.

Oh, what was she going to do?

As quickly as she asked it, she started the engine and drove off. With a sense of trepidation, she knew exactly what she must do.

Chapter 27   5

Thomas wondered if he'd imposed on Gloria too much. On Wednesday he stopped by her office after breakfast. "Frank is coming at ten, but I see you're working so that's fine. Don't—"

"Thomas." She punched a couple buttons on her computer. "Jim has already told me to go anytime. He's as jittery about this as we are."

"I'm trying not to be."

"Go on," she said. "I'll be there soon."

Gloria arrived at 9:30, soon after he'd taken a quick shower and dressed in a turtleneck and jeans that were worn just enough to be stylish. His hair was still damp. She tapped on the dining room door. "Can I come in, or do you want Frank to look first?"

"No, it's okay now. Come on in."

He'd set up three easels, one near the lighted Christmas tree and two on the other side of the fireplace. The other paintings hung on brackets around the walls, replacing those from which reproductions had been made. A table near the fireplace held the notebook of captions Gloria had edited and typed.

She began by looking at the two by the fireplace and slowly made the rounds. She faced the paintings most of the time so he couldn't see her expression. Finally, when she'd gone almost all around the room, she looked over her shoulder long enough to say, "Oh, that's Jim." She moved to the next one. "You painted Caleb. They weren't in your notes."

"They're recent additions. I have notes about Jim but not Caleb. I won't ask if I can include his story unless Frank approves this project."

He saw her nod, but she didn't turn. Maybe she remembered having praised Caleb when talking to Raymond. Thomas wanted to include a veteran, bring a renewed awareness to the public about the sacrifices they made.

She stood there a long time, silent. But one could hardly turn and smile and say paintings of homeless people were wonderful.

Then Frank appeared. He and Gloria introduced themselves before Thomas walked up to them.

Gloria offered to leave them alone and go into the living room, but Frank said that was up to Thomas. "I'd like her to stay. She edited and typed my handwritten notes for me. And she's one of the few people who knows what I've been doing for the past three years."

"Then by all means, stay," Frank said and smiled.

Gloria sat at the table, her face as bleak as Thomas felt, but he gestured around the room. "There they are."

"What's your theme, Thomas?"

"The givers and the receivers."

"You want to explain that?"

"If the paintings don't do that, the words won't."

Frank nodded. Of course, he already knew no words would alter his opinion. His assessment had indicated that when he'd told Thomas his work was similar to thousands of other painters. Good, but not distinctive.

Thomas stood in front of the fireplace, his hands clasped behind his back, while Frank made his rounds, reminding Thomas of a physician who might tell a patient he would be well in no time, or that he was sorry but he wasn't going to make it.

Gloria sat with her hands tightly clasped on the table, wide-eyed and watching Frank. There wasn't much to see but a middle-aged executive-type man in a business suit. After looking at a few, Frank said, "No frames. I've heard of this technique but haven't seen it before."

Thomas walked over to him. "It's a contemporary process called deckle edge," he explained. "I'd heard of it, but it didn't seem to suit my paintings. Then when I started this project, expense and convenience were factors. I couldn't afford frames and mats and glass. I could sketch anywhere, and when I could afford art supplies, I'd paint while in a shelter then mail my work for James to store for me."

"Looks like adversity can sometimes be a blessing." Frank glanced at him and moved on to another painting.

"I think so in this case. I'd planned to finish the project by the end of the year. Then when you said you'd be visiting I thought it might be better for you to see these here instead of my packing them up to be seen in your DC office. So again expense and convenience became factors. I didn't have the luxury to frame these in a traditional way. I tried the deckle process and realized that raw edge complements these paintings."

Frank nodded. "I totally agree. Galleries would appreciate not having to worry about scratched or broken glass and heavy pictures to hang."

"And no reflection from lights," Thomas added. "The work is simpler, and I did the edging in a couple days. Framing would have taken weeks."

Frank's glance over at him and his nod indicated that, at least, Frank was pleased with what he hadn't included. No frames, no mats, no glass. While Frank continued around the room, Thomas took a seat adjacent to Gloria. She glanced over, and he thought her tentative smile was meant to be encouraging. She then turned her attention to the notebook, opened it, and seemed to be reading what she had typed.

Finally, Frank joined them and sat opposite Gloria. She closed the notebook and slid it over to Frank who opened it. That man could be expressionless. He read each caption and a couple times he studied one more than another.

Finally he looked up, took off his glasses, and massaged the corners of his eyes with the thumb and forefinger of his right hand. Thomas was afraid to look at Gloria who seemed to have leaned over to her purse, and he feared it was to grab a tissue. He was trying to keep his own emotions out of this.

Frank gazed at him. "Which are you, Thomas. The giver or the receiver?"

"Both. All. What I'm trying to say is that we're all…everyman. Personally, I've been on the giving and receiving end."

Frank's delaying didn't make it a bit easier. Worse, if anything. Thomas remembered Gloria asking what he'd do if they were not good enough. Oh, if they weren't he could say flippant things or even rant for a while about his career being over before it got a good start. It reminded him of what Gloria said about having thought she lost her future, her security. He'd learned from her, too.

Frank tapped the notebook. "I suppose you're thinking a book with photographs of the paintings, the captions, maybe DVDs and individual flyers with photos for display, promotion, or souvenirs for the public."

"You know, Frank. That's the way I used to think—I would hit the big time. Be a recognized artist. But when I started this, I mainly wanted confirmation that I'm more than just good. I've wanted that from you. I still do," he said quickly.

"I'm not the last word, you know," Frank said.

"I know. But you know art, you know the art world, and you know the public. Your opinion is valued. But now that I've finished, I know this is the best I can do. I hope I will become an even better painter. But for now, this is everything. I know those paintings are good. I know the difference in what I did three years ago and now. Then it was my talent. Now it's my heart and soul."

Gloria seemed to be wiping her eyes and nose a lot. Frank just kept looking at him and said, "Go on."

Thomas wasn't sure what Frank wanted from him, but he suspected it wasn't just about his paintings. Frank was a no-nonsense businessman, but he was also James's father-in-law, a member of the family. He repeated to Frank some of what he'd shared with Jim and with Gloria. And as he talked, he felt like a psychologist, analyzing himself.

"I committed this project to the Lord, and to paint the homeless I'd have to be involved with them, get to know them. Then I realized that wasn't enough. I needed to *be* one of them. Feel like them. Not rely on the reproduction royalties you were holding for me. Not live in an empty hotel. Not live with James. Not get a side job. You really know another person only by walking in their shoes."

Frank and Gloria stared at him as if he were in the middle of a story and should continue. He was still learning about himself as he sat there. "I didn't intend to paint volunteers. As time went on, I saw their purpose and caring and knew they are the ones who sacrifice, bring home, show love. I needed to be a volunteer, too, and that's what I became at the center here."

He glanced at Gloria then, and she smiled. He continued, "Volunteers are the happiest people I've ever known. Well, besides my grandmother when she was making soup."

Gloria spoke up. "The ones I saw eating it were pretty happy."

He nodded. "Short-time basis though. A person can get tired of soup but never tired of one person helping another." He looked at Frank again, just a family member now, not an agent. "Those three years have led up to this day, Frank, as if it's Armageddon. But with you making me talk, I'm realizing it's not. I've learned that the recipient is a part of the giving process, too. How sad if a person could never give. If he never had an opportunity to give or use what means he has—a smile, some food, an act of kindness, an arm around the shoulder, a touch, a joke. These givers are the volunteers." Thomas shook his head. "I've learned more about God's love in shelters than I ever did when we had enough money and a thriving business."

"Sounds like your venture has been worthwhile, Thomas," Frank said.

Thomas nodded. "Maybe the purpose of these three years was not so I could be a famous artist, but maybe the Master Artist wanted to paint in my life and my heart a dependence on Him—knowledge of Him personally. There's a verse my grandmother underlined in her Bible that I remembered many times when I didn't know where I'd sleep or eat next. Something about how good it is to be near God and that I've made the Lord my shelter."

As Thomas said the words to Frank, he realized the truth of them. He'd committed three years to God, to discover what kind of artist he could be, and while he wanted the paintings to be good enough for Frank, he realized the depth of him wanted them to be good enough for God. And they were. Because he'd given his all, his best.

"If this is just my gift to God, that's fine. Because it is. It is."

"I'm glad to hear you say that, Thomas." Frank took a deep breath as if his next words would be painful.

Chapter 28

"I want to tell you a story," Frank said. He looked at Gloria. "And if that little iPhone is recording this, that's fine. You might be able to use it some way."

"Thank you," Gloria said, looking sheepish, but she lifted her phone from the chair next to her and placed it on the table. Thomas was surprised that she might have recorded their conversations.

Frank cleared his throat, looked rather miserable in fact, and began. "Many years ago in another city, we had this deacon in church. I won't go into details, but after his divorce, he was asked to step down. He'd lost wife, children, home, and eventually his job; and church people felt sorry for him and prayed for him, but we didn't really befriend him. We lost track of him, and one day the newspaper reported that he must have fallen down the slanting concrete beneath an overpass and rolled into the street just as a car was coming. From evidence, he'd been sleeping under the bridge. A homeless man. Shelters weren't plentiful there like they are in and around DC."

Frank leaned back in the chair and stared at the ceiling. Finally his troubled eyes met Thomas's again. "Why didn't we help him, Thomas? We in the church were good, decent Christian people."

He tapped the notebook with his finger. "These Christians and other caring people are doing what we should have done. We knew him. He was one of us. Fell on hard times. Many said he brought it on himself. Maybe. But we had no right to judge and accuse. We should have helped."

"It's not too late for that church to do something."

Frank huffed. "Just what I was thinking. And *each* of us is the church."

Thomas felt a bit of accomplishment. Maybe that was the purpose of over three year's work. To revive that feeling in Frank. To change one person. One person could influence others, change a church or a community. Frank was an influential man.

"Thomas, I know a little about the creative spirit. You need confirmation that your work is worthwhile. Mine is only one opinion. But I say this with all confidence: You're not an aspiring artist anymore. You are an artist." He glanced around the wall. "These paintings are real, alive, and touch the heart, and the collection should be called 'Everyman.' But…"

Thomas felt he could say it for Frank. "But who would visit a gallery to see paintings of homeless men?"

"Exactly," Frank said, nodding. "And that will be part of our promotional campaign. We'll have every art critic, every art lover, every person who's heard, and not heard, of your art ask that question. Why would any artist paint homeless people, and why would anyone want to see them?" Frank grinned. "The galleries will be bidding against each other for the first exhibit, and then the others will wait impatiently. We'll start in DC."

Thomas wasn't sure he was hearing right. But Frank kept right on. "And when they see the paintings and the books and each separate leaflet, they'll know the answer to why. They'll see themselves anew, as I did, walking around this room. They will feel again any time they've ever suffered or grieved or lost hope. And they'll also see themselves in someone simply putting food on a plate and saying an encouraging word. You do need to get into this notebook what you told me about your purpose, what you learned, what you intended."

Thomas shook his head. "I'm not even sure what all I said."

Frank looked at Gloria who picked up the cell phone and gave a little uncertain grimace. "It's on my voice recorder app."

"You have a good editor there, Thomas."

"I'm not a real editor," Gloria said. "I just edited and typed what he had in handwritten notes."

"That's what an editor does. So we'll need to see that you get paid for your editing."

"I'm a volunteer," Gloria said, going along with the theme of the hour.

"Sorry. This is business. At least, you're a freelance editor. And smart enough to know when to record what a client is saying. I often have need of a first reader or someone who can do a little editing. If you're interested, we can talk sometime."

He stood. "But right now, I have some calls to make and a few paintings to take with me. I suppose you have copies of everything in this notebook," he said to Gloria.

"On the computer."

"Then I'll take this with me, Thomas. Oh, and be sure to get either paintings or photos of you before and after."

"Before and after?" Thomas questioned.

Frank toyed with his chin. "The bush on your face. The public will want to see how you look during your project and afterwards."

Thomas lifted his hands. "I don't have photos—"

"He's in a lot of the pictures we've taken for promotion," Gloria said, "and some just for fun to put on the center's bulletin board."

Frank stood. "That will certainly speed up this process.

Gloria, could you take some photos of a few of these paintings for me? I'll see about getting this right off to a few publishing companies, along with a copy of the notebook," he explained to Thomas as if he didn't know. "There will be a bidding on this project when they know you'll be having an exhibit."

Gloria had already pulled out her camera and begun snapping. Thomas watched in wonder as those two took over his project. When he'd asked Gloria to type a few notes for him, he had no idea how invaluable she would be to this.

Now Frank was saying he'd follow Gloria to the center to get the project off and look at the photos of Thomas. One would think she'd become Frank's secretary. He wondered if Gloria realized Frank didn't make useless comments, such as about being able to use her in freelance editing projects. She might end up with two job offers to decide between, Raymond's and Frank's.

After several paintings were packed, Frank said he'd take them on out to the car and wait for Gloria. Thomas walked her to the back door and held her coat for her to slip into. "Thank you, Gloria. Your being here means the world to me."

"You're welcome," she said faintly. "And congratulations."

"Frank has said yes to representation. The galleries and publishers could still say no."

"That's not likely, is it?"

"No. But I feel good that I'd be okay if they say no. When everything looked like it was headed for no, I felt peace. I felt God was saying, 'Well done, good and faithful servant,' because that's what I've tried to be for three years. Let nothing stand in the way of using, discovering, what I am as an artist. You made the last part of this journey much more pleasant than it would have been without you. And today, you are invaluable."

She fastened the belt on her coat. "I'm glad I could be of assistance."

"That sounds so formal."

She looked up then and into his eyes. "I do mean it. I wanted to be here today because I thought you might need me. I wondered, too, who would want to see paintings of homeless people. But…" She shrugged as if she didn't know what to do with someone who appeared to be on his way to success.

He wasn't sure he did either. He'd noticed a lot of people seemed humble when in need but not so much when they seemed to have all and more than they needed.

Her eyes seemed moist as she said, "I was really touched by what you said today. I not only think you're a great artist, I very much respect and admire the kind of man you are."

The kind of man he'd become grew out of need, need for God to confirm his worth as an artist, as a human being. He hoped he'd learned lessons he'd never forget.

Over time, Gloria had accepted and liked him as a homeless volunteer. If this worked out the way Frank seemed to think, would she like him…that way? Her tone seemed to say the project was over. Her help had ended.

The project wasn't settled yet. "I still have a few loose ends." Besides signing contracts and getting monetary advances, he was thinking about the work ahead. "I'll want to talk with Caleb, get those notes typed up. Get Jim's permission to write his story about helping others follow their dreams."

She nodded. "I'll work with this as long as needed."

She'd been more excited about his hopes and dreams and being helpful than in his probable success. Now why was that? There was much he wanted to say, but Frank was out there freezing or running out of gas. Thomas longed to brush back that errant curl along the side of her face as she often did, but he willed his hand to turn the knob and open the door. "Thank you."

"You're welcome," she said and stepped outside.

"Gloria," he said, and she stopped. "Sounds like you and Frank will be working out of your office. Whatever you want to tell Jim and Clara is fine. But I need to be the one to let the others know."

She nodded and hurried to her car.

He felt the blast of cold wind on his face. He'd dared not let himself dream of anything but this project since he'd made his commitment three years ago. It was close to being over. Whether or not any contracts were signed or dreams materialized.

He would never fear homelessness again. He could live with that. But success could be more difficult to handle than failure.

Was it going to be that way for...Gloria?

192
158
34

Chapter 29

Frank and Jim were more adept on the computers than Gloria, so the two of them worked on getting the photos into the machines and matching them up with the captions. Gloria worked in the RA's office and edited Thomas's introductions, when she could see through her blurry eyes, wet with emotion of Thomas's dream so close to being realized.

By the time they finished, Frank received calls from two editors of huge companies expressing their interest. Frank told them the book manuscript was being sent around. The editors responded that they'd be taking it to committee as soon as possible. Frank hung up, and his smile was wide. "The bidding has begun."

That evening at supper, she, Jim, and Clara talked about it. Everything pointed to Thomas's three-year journey ending successfully. "He deserves it," Jim said. "He worked for it every step of the way."

"The residents are going to really miss him," Gloria said.

"Is he going away?" Clara asked.

"I don't think so. He's talked about being home. But if this works out, he probably won't have time to cook at the shelter."

Jim scoffed. "If Clara would let me, I'd bet you on that.

He's not abandoning anyone. And Gloria, you've been a big part of his life for a long time now."

"Don't try to make something personal out of this, Jim. It was all about the project."

"Really?" Jim huffed. "Well, I know as much as you about computers, and I've been decorating Christmas trees longer than either of you have been living, so why didn't he invite me to a romantic dinner in an empty hotel? With candlelight and everything?"

Clara laughed. "He probably knew I'd object."

A little humor could help. But so could honesty. "He asked me because all he needed was a little typing. And you're much busier at the center than I. But…" She felt she could be a little more honest. "I was glad to meet a need for a homeless man. Now I feel honored that I helped a great man. He is, you know."

Jim nodded. "The potential for it is there. If there's any greatness to it though, it's because of his commitment to the Lord and wanting his life and talent to be used for God's glory and the good of mankind. He acknowledges he's homeless and hopeless without the Lord."

Gloria was nodding now. "I've learned from that. And you two"—she looked from one to another—"have shown me what commitment to the Lord means. Not what you get for yourself but what you can give to others."

"Don't be too hard on yourself, Gloria. We all have to learn those things for ourselves. The good Lord gives us brains and opportunities and lets us meet people and allows us choices. We need to use what we have in making decisions. But we have to learn what seems good isn't always best. Only the Lord knows that, and we need to let him lead."

"I'm trying to learn to do that," Gloria admitted. "I didn't handle the Raymond situation well. Now I'm glad I didn't get Raymond. Glad I lost the job. Glad I lost what I thought was security. I'm even"—this she hadn't thought she could ever do—"learning to understand my parents' commitment to the mission field. It's like Thomas said, when you make a vow to the Lord, you don't back out of it." She sighed. "I've been selfish."

"There's nothing wrong with wanting your parents with you."

"You two have been all the parents anyone could want, and I love you as much or more than I love my own parents." Clara patted her hand. "Do you think my parents knew how I felt?"

"Yes," Jim said, "and that's not a bad thing. No parent wants to think their child is perfectly content without them."

"And I knew a few people who had their parents with them all the time but didn't have a good relationship or didn't appreciate them. Now that I've grown up a little I see that God gave me two sets of parents," Gloria said.

"And you're the child we never had," Clara said. "I couldn't ask for a better daughter. You're much too hard on yourself."

A few days later Frank surprised Gloria by letting her know that he and Thomas had approved the book deal offered by an editor, and the signed contracts were on their way back to the publishing company. They would work in conjunction with the gallery on getting the book published by the time of Thomas's exhibit. No contracts had been signed with the gallery, but they were in meetings deciding on the dates of the exhibit.

And then he asked if she were available to be a first reader on a manuscript a prospective writer had sent to his agency. She didn't feel qualified, but Frank's e-mail said all she needed to do was read it for interest and point out any glaring errors, any needed information the author should have included, or anything overdone. Not to worry, hers wouldn't be the final word, only the first word.

She had to cry a little, and when Jim came into the office she told him. Then later in the day, to her surprise, Thomas popped in looking the same as usual in worn jeans, a T-shirt, and the bush on his face. She cried again while telling him.

She reminded him of what she'd said about changing her major so Raymond would give her a managerial position. "But my real love was English," she said. "I thought I might teach, and way back in my mind was a possibility of writing. Never in my wildest dreams would I expect a prominent agent to ask me to read something and give my opinion." She might as well go further. "Or that I'd have any part in helping a little on a book for a famous man."

"And who is that famous man?"

She pointed at him.

He shook his head. "That was a homeless man you helped. Not a famous one. And he knows what is happening now may never happen again. We're all one bad decision or one adversity away from disaster."

She smiled at that. "And someone told me adversity can be a blessing when committed to the Lord."

"Just getting through it is a blessing," he said then smiled. "Speaking of blessings, Jim said your parents will be back soon."

"Yes, they'll be on furlough for six months."

"They're welcome to stay in an almost empty hotel."

"They're used to little grass huts"—she exaggerated a little—"so Jim and Clara's house is like a mansion to them."

"I know the feeling," he said. "Now I have an appointment with Caleb. Did you know Ted hired him?"

"I heard that. He and Heather and Bobby are planning to be together again by Christmas."

"Thanks again, for everything," he said as he left.

She thought of the difference in her thinking since a few months ago. There were still things she wanted for herself. But instead of dwelling on what may not be God's plan for her, she was truly happy for Thomas and his success, that his dream was coming true. She was thrilled with Caleb getting a job and being with his family again.

Her thoughts concentrated more on her blessings now. Her

parents were coming home. Some desires of her heart were happening, some, like with Frank, that she didn't even know had been in her heart.

She would not fuss about what other dreams might be in her heart. It wasn't always best to get what you want, like her life of security with Raymond. She didn't have to always like it, but she would just…trust God, who knew best.

Thomas invited her, Clara, Jim, and the volunteers to supper the following week when he'd cook for the residents. After they served the residents, they all stayed, and Thomas told them about the project, how he'd been on the streets and decided to bring more awareness of homelessness to the public. He praised Gloria for the time and work she'd put into the book, and they applauded. When he said Jim and Caleb would be included in the book and paintings, they all clapped and whistled, having taken a liking to Caleb and his family.

He stressed the adversities in his life and about his living in an empty hotel. He would be needing some laborers to clean, make any minor repairs that might be required, do yard work, wash windows, and address anything else necessary to make it more habitable. Their response was wonderful.

After his speech Thomas sat in the chair Jim had saved for him, between him and Lois's husband. "You should tell your story to the church," Jim said.

"Oh yes," Lois readily agreed. "They need to be reminded we can always use more donations and volunteers. They're used to me, but they'd listen to an artist."

Thomas looked past her husband. "They'd listen to you if you waved that spatula around at them instead of at me."

"Tell me about it!" her husband said, and they all laughed.

"Seriously though," Thomas said, "I'd like to do that. Speaking to churches should be a natural outgrowth of the project, which is not to promote myself but bring attention to the needs, the goodness of people, and the opportunities."

"It would be a great tribute to your dad," Jim said. "And

a time to say how much the workers and volunteers mean to the homeless."

"Right," Thomas agreed. "We," he said with a nod toward Gloria, "have included the church in the acknowledgments since they sponsor Wildwood."

Lois pushed back from the table. "Looks like they've just about got everything cleaned up, so it's time I asked if I can do anything." She said she was so proud of Thomas and Gloria then lifted her hands. "All of you."

"And we of you, Lois," Jim said, and they all nodded.

After they left, Thomas said, "Before you three leave, I have something for you."

He went behind the kitchen counter and returned with three envelopes with their names in beautiful script. One for Jim and Clara, one for Mr. and Mrs. Seely, and one for Gloria.

She thought the envelopes would hold an invitation to his art exhibit or announce the publication date of his book. After they walked home, Gloria and Clara hastily extracted the flap out of the envelopes and removed the folded cards—and they gasped, giving each other a surprised, wide-eyed look.

Chapter 30

"Let me see yours," Clara said at the same time Gloria reached for hers.

"I want in on this, too," Jim said, as he opened the one to the Seelys.

"That's a federal offense," Clara warned. "Let me see."

They all exchanged the cards. On the front in beautiful red script were the words *A Party for My Friends*. On Gloria's was a small sketch of her with a tinge of watercolor for emphasis. Sketches of Jim and Clara graced theirs.

"How did he know what my parents look like?"

"Oh," Clara said, "he stopped by one evening when you went to the movies with Heather and Marge. We got to talking about them, so I showed him my picture album."

"You didn't tell me that."

"Well hon, should I?" She got that playful look. "You weren't taking him personally."

"Claraaaaa," she scolded, while Jim chuckled. "Maybe we should look inside and see when this party takes place."

They opened the cards, and inside a few words provided details. There would be a drop-in reception for a few friends at the hotel following the Singing Christmas Tree program at the church. He asked that they park at the back and enter that way, since he didn't want it to appear the hotel was open for business.

That would be two weeks before Christmas.

In the meantime her parents arrived, and they had a wonderful time becoming reacquainted, as adults appreciating each other's lives and work. They wanted to see the shelter the next day, so all of them ate breakfast at Wildwood, met Thomas, and thanked him for the invitation.

They were proud of Gloria's accomplishments with Thomas's book and her work at the shelter. "I don't deserve praise," she said. "You two went to the mission field willingly. I didn't have much of a choice when I started working here. But God was in it."

"We didn't always go willingly, Gloria," her dad said, and her mom put her arm around Gloria's waist. "We never wanted to leave you. But it wasn't best you go with us except in your early years. You got a better high school and college education here and the loving care from Clara and Jim that you deserved."

"Thank you for your sacrifice," she said. She'd learned to appreciate their life of service.

They left with Clara, but Jim and Gloria stayed to work in the office. Her thoughts however turned to that upcoming Singing Christmas Tree event and the party and wondering what to wear.

The invitation had said a few friends. One of his friends was a millionaire. Her parents were missionaries, but they had nice clothes they left at Clara and Jim's since they were often asked to speak in churches when they were on furlough. Finally she decided to dress like she did before coming to live with Jim and Clara and working in a homeless shelter, and felt good about it.

On the day of the party, she washed her hair and used a curling iron to give it an extra flair. She dressed in the outfit she'd bought last Christmas for what she'd thought would be the special occasion of becoming engaged. Now she would wear it in celebration of not becoming engaged.

It was a short, black satin party dress that fell right above her knees. The waistline was decorated with silver rhinestones as were the straps fastened to the straight neckline bordered by a row of rhinestones. She knew it was classy and wore long, dangling rhinestone earrings and satin three-inch heels. Since Jim would drive them to the church, she wouldn't wear a coat, but the black satin shawl.

Gloria had attended the Singing Christmas Tree program in years past. It was quite famous around the area. They were all delighted with it as usual, especially her parents who didn't get to come home every Christmas.

Many people at the church came up to speak to her parents after the program. By the time they arrived at the hotel, a couple cars were parked out back. A car pulled in right after Jim. Pastor Dan and his wife, Norma, exited the front of the car. Caleb and Heather got out of the back.

They walked to the back door and as soon as it was opened, a woman welcomed them, asked for their coats, and hung them in a nearby closet. Caleb looked nice in a suit and tie. Heather wore a lovely strapless dress with a white bodice and green skirt. They complimented each other on their looks.

The woman asked that they go into the dining room, help themselves to appetizers, and continue on to the living room.

Ted, in a formal suit and bow tie, and Libby, wearing a beautiful red cocktail dress that complemented her dark hair, gathered goodies on their plates while Blackston answered questions about the treats and took orders for the drinks of their choice.

Glancing around the wall, Gloria noticed the paintings from which reproductions for tourists had been made hung back in their places. The paintings of homeless and volunteers were probably at the gallery.

As soon as they entered the living room, she recognized James but not the good-looking man talking to him. Until he turned his head and his dark eyes met hers. That was Thomas, his eyes dancing, moving his hand up to his smoothly shaved face, looking like he was…handsome or something.

He came over. All she could think to say was, "Do I know you?"

"Better than anyone else here," he said. "I don't believe you've formally met James." He made the introductions that included Arlene, a pretty woman wearing an elegant, long ivory-colored dress. She also met Frank's wife, Jan, an attractive woman in silk formal pants and a gold metallic top.

Everyone looked so beautiful. The setting and everything seemed so perfect, so different from the shelter. Then she almost laughed. She wasn't exactly wearing jeans and a T-shirt either.

"Looks like we're all here," Thomas said. "When anyone wants seconds, there's Blackston to help you." Blackston stood at the doorway. "Then let's have a seat and get reacquainted."

Chapter 31

Four each sat on the couches. Easy chairs sat alongside.
Thomas began by saying he wanted to share with them what
he'd been doing for three years.

Gloria sank into one of the easy chairs, watching and listening to Thomas talk. He told the same story she already
knew but never tired of hearing. His emphasis was different
than when he talked to Frank. He now included Caleb, who
was beginning to accept the trauma and understand that he
was a hero, like any fighting man. He'd been spending time
with his family and would move back in with them during
the coming week.

Her parents talked about their missionary experiences,
some harrowing, but most delightful, about the small church
that was growing, and people coming to know the Lord.

Frank praised Gloria's work on the notebook and the manuscript she'd helped with, saying, "I'm sure there will be many
more if you're willing. Whether they would be plentiful or
sparse is unpredictable. In the arts, not much is guaranteed."

Thomas agreed. "This upcoming exhibit may be the only
one I ever have. Can't count on another."

"It's a little different with you now, Thomas," Frank said.

"The promotion is already going out. You're becoming known. After this you can paint"—he spread his hands—"flowers if you like, and they'll be acclaimed and sold."

"You make it sound like something's wrong with flowers."

Frank reared back. "Not at all. Monet did all right."

They all agreed with that.

"I prefer faces," Thomas said, "but flowers are not a bad idea. I've watched the flowers that Gloria raises and brings to the shelter. They wilt and die. I see the pansies and think of them returning another year. An evening primrose blooms in the evening, but the blooms wither and fall off the following morning. A coneflower or a daisy or daffodil will return year after year. Crocuses pop up through the snow. The theme could be, as my editor told me," he said and grinned, looking at Gloria, "that you need to bloom where you're planted. You don't know if your purpose is short or long term."

Gloria shook her head. "Clara's the one who told me that."

Clara shrugged. "My sister told me."

Gloria's mom laughed. "I think the saying has been around for a while."

Frank sighed. "Just can't stop those creative minds."

"But," Thomas said, "before I seriously consider flowers, I've been thinking about Mr. and Mrs. Seely's description of those needy little children and how their eyes are haunting. Paintings of them and the missionaries who sacrifice to give them physical and spiritual life sounds to me like a worthy theme."

Gloria could think of only one night that could top this one and that was when she and Thomas had sat in there alone. Everyone in the group related well. Thomas's friends and her family.

Ted could be serious, but he also was a joker and soon had them all laughing while Libby gazed at him like he was the cat's meow. He entertained them with Christmas jokes and true stories, like his getting stuck in a pipe. He had everyone laughing.

Blackston rolled in a cart laden with goodies and drinks. Several of the group went over, including Gloria to refill her glass. Next thing she knew she heard Ted exclaim, "Look who's standing where?"

Everyone looked, and he held mistletoe over her head and that of the person standing next to her. Thomas!

Libby poked Ted. "I told you not to do that." Everyone seemed to still be in the lighthearted and fun mood that Ted had set. Thomas was the hero of the night, but Ted was the life of the party. This fit in naturally with what Ted would do, and with her and Thomas being the only single persons there.

Gloria didn't know what to do. Just laugh and lean forward for Thomas to lightly touch her lips with his? Right here in front of all these people? She kept the smile pasted on her face but didn't meet Thomas's eyes. To back away and say no would put tension into the festivities, and what kind of impression would it give? That she didn't want to kiss Thomas and embarrass him? That she did and was afraid it would look too serious? Or too trivial? This was supposed to be a silly, fun time.

Thomas seemed hesitant, too. He said something silly to Ted, and everyone laughed. Then Thomas said, "My grandmother always told me, remember who you are. You're a Knight, so behave like one. So, in deference to my grandmother, I shall give the fair lady a proper kiss."

He reached for her hand, lifted it, and pressed his lips to the back of it. Then he made a mock bow, and she had no choice but to laugh lest she cry. She felt color rise in her cheeks and forced a smile. She tried to curtsey, and it must have looked something like one because they all applauded.

Ted said, "Guess I'll have to show you how it's done." He moved over to Libby and held the mistletoe over them, and

Libby eagerly obliged for their sweet kiss. "Now," Libby said, "get rid of that before we get thrown out of here."

"Back where I got it." He stuck the fake mistletoe into his jacket pocket. Everyone turned to the food and drink. Heather said something to Gloria about the coconut macaroons to which Gloria replied, she wasn't sure with what, but she didn't want a macaroon, only something to moisten her dry throat.

Everyone was busy with food and drink and conversation and had no reason to give further thought to the funny little incident by which they'd been entertained. But she was thinking only someone like Thomas could pull off what he did and make a flopped play look like a smash hit. He had a creative flair. Eccentric. The audience liked the twist instead of the expected. But she knew, even if no one else did, Thomas did not want to kiss her. Not even in a playful way. Not even a little innocent peck.

Chapter 32 3

Where do I go from here? Gloria wondered

Arlene said she'd like to look at the ornaments on the Christmas trees. James replied he hadn't seen them in over three years.

"James, you maybe know what some of them mean more than I do since you're older," Thomas said.

James gave him a mock-mean look at the older remark.

Thomas just laughed. "There's another tree with ancient ornaments in the dining room."

"Jim and I have been here for dinner around Christmastime," Clara said. "I'd love to hear about the ornaments." James led the way. Jim, Clara, Gloria's parents, Frank's wife, and Arlene followed him. Ted, Libby, Caleb, and Heather returned to the couches. Gloria thought of sitting with them but heard them start talking about their children. Thomas and Frank stood off to one side, so she strolled around, looked at the decorations, admired the crèche, moved to the front window, and peeked out. She thought that might be a few flakes of snow.

She walked over to the glass doors that opened into the entry then unlocked the front door and went out onto the porch. She set her glass on the banister and put her hands on the railing. The sparsely falling snow began to lie on the ground.

Not wanting to entertain negative thoughts, she thanked God that she'd learned so much in the past months. She had job opportunities now, but even if she didn't, she could stay with Clara and Jim as long as needed, help at the shelter, and feel she had purpose. *Your will, Lord. I willed Raymond, and he wasn't best.*

She heard the door open and the screen squeak. Someone else was coming to watch the snow fall. Feeling a chill, she hugged her arms and looked over her shoulder. Then Thomas stood beside her. They both held on to the railing.

"Gloria," he said, and the sound was like the softly falling snow. "I haven't kissed a girl in over three years. I don't intend to play at life anymore, which means I'm not even going to play at kissing because someone prompts me. I know it would have been fun, but I didn't want it to be something in jest."

"Oh, that's fine." She shrugged.

"I understand those who enjoy having a little fun with things like that, and I see nothing wrong with it. But it would have been wrong for me."

She hoped her smile had frozen.

"And another reason—"

She turned. "Thomas. Stop! You don't have to explain. What's a stupid little kiss under some…some…fake parasitical berries? Even in fun?"

He put his hands on her shoulders and turned her toward him. "Another reason is because I wanted to." His voice stayed soft. "My first kiss in over three years mustn't be just for fun or so casual. I may even have forgotten how."

She was thinking that she might only be a typist, but perhaps she could help him.

She could not look away. His face came closer. The warm breath in the cold air was on her lips, followed by his own.

They were warm, tender, moving against hers, making her eyes close, her arms go around his neck, and her heart beat against his, and her lips felt as if they'd been lonely all her life, until now.

Finally, he moved back, but she could still feel the wonder of the kiss.

She stared into his eyes for a long time and finally found her voice. "You haven't forgotten how."

His smile was as warm as his gaze. "Wouldn't have mattered. This was unlike any of the others anyway. I don't care to remember any of them."

She smiled right back. This time she didn't think she'd lost her mind.

She'd lost her heart.

They turned to watch the snow for a moment. She remembered he said there was more than one kind of kiss. She didn't need a dictionary to figure this one out. Of course it was a physical act. And they were two single people. He hadn't had female companionship in three years. And the last kiss she vividly remembered was the one Raymond and Stephanie shared in the storeroom back in February.

My goodness, why *shouldn't* she and Thomas share one, too? They'd worked together, gotten to know each other, shared the negative and positive things about their lives. They'd come to…like each other.

A man should be kissed at his own party when celebrating a huge success and with a great future ahead of him and on a softly falling snowy kind of evening. And, too, she'd been *lovely* in her green sundress. This was black satin with rhinestones and the snow was on her shoulders and in her glass… .

She lifted her hand to brush away the snow, and he helped.

"Your guests will be wondering what happened to us."

He nodded. "I can almost hear the whispers and see the raised eyebrows. But if they were more important than you, I would still be in there instead of having come out here to you."

He moved to the front door with the Closed sign on it. He could open a wooden and glass door, and she could choose whether or not to walk inside. But one couldn't walk into another's heart without their invitation.

Someday, when she was an older spinster, she'd take her nieces and nephews to an art gallery and create in them a love for painting. And she would think about having been kissed by a famous artist, even if it was…only physical. She would never forget. He was sensitive, kind, gallant, rather like one of those chivalrous fellows who rode on a white horse.

He was a Knight to remember.

192
176
16

Chapter 33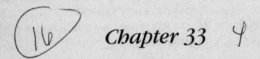

Thomas wasn't sure how to handle his feelings for Gloria. He didn't know whether he was moving too fast by having kissed her, although he didn't regret that. Or if he was moving too slow. However, his life had changed drastically and many demands were being made on it. His time wasn't his own yet.

He had many obligations to fulfill. A few days after his party, there were the holiday activities for the Wildwood residents. He didn't want them to feel he would abandon them, and he continued his cooking and providing special dishes and joined in their festivities.

In conversation he mentioned in Gloria's hearing that he'd be spending much of Christmas Day with James's family, which included being there for opening presents, and Frank, who would be talking business regardless. He was going to invite her, but she said she was looking forward to spending Christmas with her parents and Jim and Clara.

"You have plans for Christmas Eve?" he asked.

"Not really. Other than being with family."

"Would you like to attend a Christmas carol concert in Silver City?"

"Sounds nice."

He told her the time and thought he should add, "I have a little present for you." He had his forefinger and thumb about half an inch apart and decided to be more specific. "Well, not that little." He formed a square with his hands about 3x4 inches. "But it's just a small thing."

He didn't want to give any false impressions. Last Christmas she'd expected a ring from her boyfriend and was later devastated. Not that she was expecting or wanting anything from him.

She laughed lightly. "I have a little present for you, too." She formed a square about 2x4 inches. "And thicker than yours." She measured about two inches with her finger and thumb.

After the concert they went to the Percolator for coffee. He gave her his present first. She slowly loosened the taped paper, and the smile faded the moment she saw it. He thought the gold-jeweled, ornate picture frame was perfect for the small painting. "Oh," she whispered. "This is wonderful, Thomas. It's like the sketch you made on their invitation. Except this is a painting, not a sketch."

"I got several pictures of your parents from Clara."

She looked at it lovingly then at him. With her looking at him like that, he thought he perhaps should have given it to her on the porch of the hotel. On second thought, this was safer.

"I truly love it," she said and held it to her heart for a moment, and then she looked at it again. She sighed. "Compared with this, my present is…silly."

"No present is silly."

She slid it from her purse, and he tore off the paper. He gasped, looking at the box. He took out the Christmas ornament, a knight in full armor brandishing his sword.

She spoke self-consciously. "The sword is supposed to represent your paintbrush."

He looked across at her. "Do you remember what I said about my grandmother saying to remember who I am?"

She nodded. "That's why I thought of this." She made a little huff. "I told you it was silly."

"No way," he said. "It's perfect. Something I will set out to remind me who I am and what I should be." He reached over and took her hand that rested on the table. He brought it to him as he leaned over and held it and kissed the back of it. "Thank you."

At the Christmas party she'd had a fake smile and didn't meet his eyes. Her smile now was not fake, and her gaze met his, but he detected a hint of uncertainty.

But he smiled at her and soon drove her home. She said, "Don't get out," so he didn't walk her to the door and kiss her good night. Because he wanted to so very much.

Christmas Day with James's family was fun and exciting. Four-year-old Valerie was a great age for delighting in all that Christmas was about, from the story of baby Jesus to opening presents that made her eyes as big and shiny as the baubles on the tree.

Blake loved it, too, and had to be put into a playpen to keep him out of things. It was obvious Frank and Jan spoiled their grandchildren. During dinner James said, "I should apologize, Thomas. At times I've thought of you in terms of the Prodigal Son."

"That's okay," Thomas said. "I looked at you as the stodgy, pious, judgmental, older son."

"Thanks."

"Anytime."

"But you're not prodigal. You've done a good thing, finding a purpose, not giving up. I admire you for that. I followed my dream, but I didn't take chances."

Thomas nodded. "Maybe that's why I could. I knew you'd be here for me."

"Yes, I would. And you'd take me in if needed."

"Yeah James, I would. Or at least put you in a loony bin and make sure you get a little food once in a while."

James laughed. "I always knew I could count on you." He grew serious and looked at the painting over the fireplace. "You did that painting of Mom and Dad. While they were alive, I didn't think much of it. Now it's one of my most prized possessions."

Thomas looked away from him, but James brought his attention back to him. "Thomas, I know you felt like Dad had his heart attack because he lost his money." He shook his head. "You didn't stick around for the autopsy report. He died because of his heart condition. He would have even if he hadn't lost his money."

"I should have known that," Thomas said. "He loved us. I think that was just a way of handling my grief. I had to do something besides miss him so much." He tried to shake away the emotions threatening to overwhelm him.

Instead of concentrating on a past that couldn't be revived, he needed to think about his family right here. "James, with all that's going on with me, I could use a good attorney."

"I happen to know one," James said. "I would be honored."

Thomas felt like he'd really come home. And yet, something was missing. He had plenty to do, but no huge painting projects to work on, although Ted wanted a family portrait, and Frank was getting requests for portraits, too.

But he had to get on canvas what his photographic memory wouldn't forget. The beautiful woman in a black dress on the porch with snow in her hair and on her shoulders. A black-and-white picture except for her gray eyes with a touch of blue that held a hint of uncertainty, as if questioning who and what they were to each other. And the slight tinge of color in her cheeks from the cold. Or was it from inner warmth? The coral lips that had not protested when he had not resisted their lure.

He wandered into the living room where a fire glowed in the cozy room. His mind and heart filled with memories. Of his friends and family. And yet, he felt a chill as if he were out there in the icy rain. The room was empty.

However, he counted his numerous blessings. In ways he couldn't have known, while wandering the streets, the New Year looked very promising for his career.

New Year?

A stab of concern raced through his mind.

He might be too late.

192
181
11

Chapter 34   3

The next morning right after the men were served breakfast, Thomas went into the office and stood at the back of Gloria's computer. She looked up with uncertainty in her eyes, eyes that matched her blue sweater. The lips were coral, as he remembered.

"Did you take the bookstore job?"

He must look as pale as he felt. She said, "Pull up the chair, Thomas."

He did and sat opposite her.

She shook her head. "It was tempting, but I felt like I'd be taking steps backward to the way my life was before. I've learned to be"—she paused—"a giver and a receiver. Like you said, the givers are among the happiest people. I need to think seriously about God's plan for my life. It may be at a bookstore, but I don't know that right now. So I'll give here at Wildwood, and I'll receive from Clara and Jim. That makes them happy."

Painting a picture was a lot easier than finding the right words to say. "Will you go to the hotel with me?"

She stared like he'd lost his mind, but he heard someone step into the room and Jim's voice said, "She can go now if she wants to. There's not much work going on right now and the RA is helping more."

She got her jacket and went with him. When they went inside the hotel he said, "I'd like to show you all the rooms."

He showed her one bedroom on the second floor and said the others were like it. They went into his studio, and she glanced at the pictures on the easels and noticed the clutter on the tables, although that was his filing system.

"Amazing that a person can be creative in"—she grinned—"such a mess."

"It's up here and here." He touched his temple then his chest. "Just like the book you and Frank created with a camera, a screen, and a keyboard."

Yes, whether one wore a black satin dress in the snow or a blue sweater or a T-shirt and jeans, the important things were in the head and heart.

He led her into the suite and its sitting room. "This is lovely," she said of the room, and then she walked over to the bay window and said the view was beautiful.

He stood beside her and gazed out. Snow lay on the bare-limbed cherry trees and whitened the ground.

She glanced at him. "Thomas, have you been interviewing me for a job in your hotel?"

He said, "Yes." Her face turned from him, and her shoulders rose with a deep breath.

"I love you, Gloria." He heard the release of her breath, and she faced the view. "I want to offer a permanent position here in the hotel, as my wife."

"No." She turned toward him then. "I don't want a job in a hotel."

Now it was his turn to take a deep breath and hold it. He read that face wrong. Assumed too much.

But then her eyes and voice no longer held uncertainty. "I can't take the job offer. I'd rather be a volunteer."

Did she mean…at Wildwood? At the hotel?

His eyes questioned, and hers began to dance. "I want to be with you wherever you are, whatever you're doing. If you have to sleep in an alley again, just make sure there's enough room for me."

"I do have an empty hotel." He put his hands on her shoulders. "It's really true that this acclaim I'm getting may never happen again. Even if it does, there's no guarantee—"

"I know that."

He moved the errant lock of hair aside, and she lifted her face as he lowered his. Their lips touched, sealing their commitment to a life together. He did not let his lips linger too long, because...he wanted to so much.

They moved apart, and he said, "Was that a yes?"

"Definitely."

"Come," he said. "I want to show you something." When they reached the living room, she gasped to see the painting over the mantel. There stood the picture of her in the black satin dress in the snow with her eyes revealing what he had hoped was love, although that hint of uncertainty accompanied it.

"You're wonderful," she said.

He looked at the little knight in his armor she'd given him for Christmas that sat on the mantel beneath the painting. His grandmother said remember who you are and behave accordingly. The Bible said put on the armor of God so that you won't be defeated but will stand strong in the face of adversity.

"Gloria." He turned to her. "I've already committed my life and my painting to the Lord. I kept that commitment to painting for three years."

She nodded and smiled.

"Now I'm committing my life to you, too, above my painting. I expect that to be a lot easier than those three years. You look and smell better than some I've encountered in alleys."

"Thanks a lot," she said.

"Now, let's go look at rings."

She touched her head and her heart.

"I know," he said. "But let's look at rings anyway."

192
185
———
7

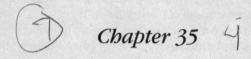

Chapter 35 4

Thomas never failed to surprise her. The ring was no surprise. They'd looked at them together, and he gave her one of several she couldn't choose from. He did that on New Year's Eve as they sat in the only place they had to be alone, and that was the hotel living room.

He'd made snacks and turned on the TV. They settled on the couch to watch the Times Square ball drop in New York City and talk about plans for their future.

He surprised her by saying, "Let's date."

"Date?" They just got engaged to be married.

"Yes, go places. The shelter and the homeless and the volunteers are in our hearts and minds to stay. They're part of us and we of them. But there's the other side of life, too. The beauty of God's creation. The hopes and aspirations of mankind."

"Now that sounds academic." She popped another piece of popcorn into her mouth.

He smiled. "I didn't appreciate the history of this area until I took the local history class under Dr. Woodrow Lawing. He's a bachelor who has devoted his life to his teaching and his students. He taught by taking us to see the sites of DC. I was thinking you and I might tour DC and surrounding areas as part of our honeymoon. But I decided I'd like to do it now."

She squealed and threw a piece of popcorn at him. "You mean, have the honeymoon before the wedding?"

"Hey, don't tempt me," he said as playfully as she had made her statement. "Let's bloom where we're planted for a while."

"I like that," she said.

"Okay. So I will plan the pre-wedding...outing, and you decide where we spend our honeymoon."

"Well, that depends on how much money...*we* have."

He shook his head. "No way. I'm not going to chance that. I think you liked me better homeless and shaggy than successful and good looking."

"What am I going to do with you?"

"Marry me, that's what."

She looked at the TV for a moment then turned to him again. "It's not that I liked you better. After I got the idea of security out of me, I wanted to be with you even if we had to survive on my minimum wage and live in an empty hotel."

"Hmmm," he said, as if that wasn't a bad idea.

"But when you made it as an artist, and now with the book, I thought there might not be a place in your life for me, personally."

"Did you ever notice I dragged you along with me everywhere?"

"I thought it was because I had a small part with your book. You were kind."

"I struggled to keep you out of my mind because I had that prior commitment. But you kept haunting me since the first time we met at the creek and you wanted to save me from diving into the water."

She smiled. "You saved me instead. You've been in my thoughts and life since I saw that gleam in your eyes when I splashed water on your face."

And so they watched the ball fall and the New Year come

in with all its promise. In the days to follow, whenever weather permitted and roads weren't cluttered with cars left stuck in the snow, they began to…date.

They visited the monuments and the Smithsonian museums to remember the greatness of America and the principles on which it was built. And the Hill. "Did you know," Thomas said, "where the Capitol stands was once a swamp off the Potomac River?"

"No, I didn't."

"Well, it was. And it can teach us a lesson. We may at times think we're living in a swamp, as I did one night trying to sleep in a smelly, hard, cold alley. The sky was threatening to give me a bath. But every once in a while the moon peeked out as if to wink and say, swamp today, Capitol tomorrow. And then I could lie there and laugh and be accepted by the rest of the homeless."

"I love the way you make an analogy out of everything, a lesson learned."

He grinned. "And did you know it's required by federal law that no building be taller than the Capitol?"

"I do now, and that reminds me there should be no gods put before God, not even…ourselves."

"Now we're communicating."

They went to Old Town Alexandria and visited the unique shops, art studios, and small galleries, and they tried the ethnic restaurants, having a choice of Chinese, Vietnamese, Indian, Thai, Latin American, African, and European.

They visited the Bonsai Gardens at the national arboretum, admiring the miniature plants, some hundreds of years old.

Finally, March came, bringing warmer weather, and so they viewed the trees surrounding places like the Washington Monument. The buds were getting ready to burst into bloom.

"I'll take you to see a different view," Thomas said. "The observation platform." From there they looked over all of DC and part of Virginia and Maryland. But most breathtaking was standing 500 feet up and looking down on the cherry trees.

"Have you decided on the honeymoon?"

"I've thought of several possibilities. But you help me on this."

"Okay," he said. "I've been to Paris. A romantic city. Has everything from little sidewalk cafés to the Eiffel Tower, and there are boat rides on the Seine." He grinned. "The Louvre, of course. Your turn."

She nodded. Since he was thinking abroad, she suggested, "Medieval castles and famous gardens of Europe."

"Hawaiian Islands with their swaying palms and hula girls."

"Ahem." She cleared her throat. "Israel and seeing what God called the most beautiful place on earth and walking where Jesus walked and going out on the Sea of Galilee and riding a camel."

She stopped talking. He was staring at her. "I like that very much."

"Jim and Clara have sponsored Israeli children for many years. They've always talked about going. But it's expensive."

"We could take them with us. Your parents, too. Maybe Jim and Clara could visit some of the children they sponsored. Maybe I could—"

"Paint them," she said at the same time as he. "Oh Thomas. That would be so wonderful."

"And we could take along one of the younger couples we know," he said. "James and Arlene wouldn't leave the children that long."

"What about Ted and Libby? They're such fun. Had it not been for Ted we wouldn't have had that first kiss."

"Not so. I had in mind to have you stay after the party. And I planned to kiss you if you'd let me. I wanted to sooner but thought you wouldn't want to kiss a man with a bush on his face." He gazed at her. "Would you?"

"I didn't exactly think it, but I was aware when I sprinkled water on your beard that you had nice lips and a great smile."

"You mean I could have been kissing you all along?"

"No. I just mean I was…aware. It's not the same."

Thomas's eyes brightened. "Ted has a private jet, too."

"And they can take a nanny along for their baby if they want."

"You wouldn't mind sharing your honeymoon with all those people?"

"I don't think we're going to be alone no matter where we go. So why not have friends and relatives in the next room instead of strangers? I love that idea."

"Anyway, I expect our honeymoon to last a lifetime. We can have an empty hotel all to ourselves for a while before we leave on the trip."

"I like that, too. We can look out on our own cherry blossom trees."

"My thoughts exactly," he said with a teasing gleam in his eyes.

Chapter 36

Spring came with all its beauty. Gloria stood at the third-floor bay window in the sitting room looking down on the cherry blossom trees in full bloom. Along with Thomas's creative ideas, she'd chosen a cherry blossom theme.

Her mother gave the final smoothing touch to the fingertip veil. "Now turn around and let me look. Oh darling, you're so beautiful."

Gloria felt beautiful. Love could do that to a person and especially when their beloved groom-to-be had said it. She'd chosen a long silk organza strapless dress, simply elegant, and carried a large bouquet of peonies, ranunculus, sweet peas, petite jasmines, and cherry blossoms.

Her mother said a short prayer with her before going downstairs to await the bride's descent down the three flights of stairs. They'd agreed on a small wedding of their closest friends, those who had attended Thomas's Christmas party. They would have receptions at Wildwood and at the church after returning from their Israel trip. Maybe a drop-in reception at the hotel and any gift ideas would be donated to a shelter.

For now, however, she heard the wedding march. The piano

had been moved near the glass doors so Clara could play and watch her come down the stairs.

She walked down, touching the railing lest she stumble if her emotions got the better of her. At the bottom of the stairs, waiting for her, stood Thomas in a formal suit and bow tie, and a wearing a cherry blossom bud boutonnière. Frank was taking pictures.

Their friends and family stood in the foyer. When she reached the lowest step, Thomas winked at her and turned to go into the living room. The others followed. Her dad held out his arm and escorted her into the living room where Jim stood in front of the fireplace to perform the ceremony. Thomas reached for her hand, and they turned toward Jim.

The words were beautiful. They repeated their vows after Jim. When she expected, "Now I pronounce you man and wife," it didn't come. Thomas took a step away from her. Softly, piano music sounded and Thomas began singing, "Unforgettable."

She'd never felt such a wonderful feeling sweeping through her as she stared into his eyes and he sang the love song. Words like *forever…incredible…someone unforgettable thinks that I am, too.*

Jim pronounced them husband and wife. Their friends and family applauded, and Ted whistled. The guests were steered toward the dining room for chocolate and cherry wedding cake.

Thomas's hand held her back. When the others had gone, he drew her to him, and they shared their first private kiss as husband and wife. It was all and more than when they stood on the porch in the snow.

"You said," she teased, "there were two kinds of kisses."

He nodded.

"What was that one?"

He scowled. "I can't say. We might have to try it again."

She pulled on his coat sleeve and for an instant glimpsed the painting over the mantel and the knight beneath it.

He had said this is where she belonged. She knew that was true. He sang that she was forever unforgettable.

And she knew he was forever her Knight to remember.

* * * * *